Troubled in Paradise

Longing for Home Book 2

Lisa Stanbridge

Crystal Brook
Publishing

Trigger Warning: This novel contains references to a child who is a result of rape, and references to brain tumours and related medical treatments, which may be triggering or upsetting for some readers.

TROUBLED IN PARADISE

Copyright © 2023 by Lisa Stanbridge

The moral right of the author has been asserted

ISBN: 978-0-6456673-2-5

Also By Lisa Stanbridge

Longing for Home series:

Lonely in Paris – Book 1

Troubled in Paradise – Book 2

Finding Our Home – Book 3

Standalone books:

Abandoned Hearts

Navigate to the link below to read more about her books.

https://lisastanbridge.wixsite.com/lisastanbridgeauthor/books

For Bree – thank you for all the fun times

Chapter 1

Jane

I love Jacques DuPont and I want to be with him forever.

Glancing across at him, I smile as he neatly packs his suitcase for our trip back to Australia. He unfolds every article of clothing he takes out of the wardrobe, then refolds a specific way for the suitcase. He says it's about saving space.

Turning to my chest of drawers, I remove a handful of clothes and dump them on the bed. Not caring about neatness or space, I check out each piece. The ones I'm taking I throw in the case; the ones I'm leaving here I throw behind me.

Sensing eyes on me, I look up to catch Jacques staring.

"What?" I dump my swimwear into the case.

"*Ooh la la*, I cannot watch you pack." He shudders and turns back to meticulously folding a dress shirt.

I chuckle and focus on packing, my thoughts drifting.

People say the first twelve months of a relationship are the hardest. You're getting to know someone. Learning their quirks and bad habits. I expected life with Jacques to be difficult considering our different circumstances. Namely the language barrier, cultural differences, and the scars from his toxic family.

But it hasn't been hard at all. If anything, it's been easy.

Almost *too* easy.

His English has improved, as has my French, so we rarely misunderstand each other. We speak English around each other, so that helps. And since we're both open to trying and experiencing new things, there are never any issues over doing something different.

We also have so many little things in common, the kind that may cause unnecessary arguments. Like, we both put the toilet seat down, hang our towels up, are neat freaks—unless I'm packing, of course—and always clean up after ourselves. Just to name a few.

Then the kicker, since cutting ties with his family, he's so much more carefree and comfortable within himself.

That's not to say we don't have our little tiffs, because we do. Over money believe it or not. And not the lack thereof. Ironic, huh?

The issue is, Jacques has expensive taste. I don't.

I'm not against money or having nice things. Far from it. We have many things I enjoy, I just don't think we always need to spend top dollar. This is an area we're still finding our feet on. After all, we were both raised so differently. It's not something we can easily change.

Despite our little tiffs, we've stuck to our promise to always communicate with each other, talk about our issues, and resolve them quickly. I don't have a single regret and the last twelve months have been the best of my life.

Another tut cuts through my thoughts. I glance up at Jacques with a grin. His eyes are wide as he takes in the growing pile of clothes behind me.

"It is all so disorganised and messy." He smiles weakly.

"Hey, I'm very tidy, thank you. Just not when I'm packing."

"That may be so, but I still cannot watch."

"Then don't." I hold his gaze as I throw a blouse over my shoulder. "It's not like you have to share my suitcase or clean up after me."

"*Dieu merci pour cela.*"

Thank goodness for that he said, and I narrow my eyes at him. "Hey, we agreed to speak English at home remember?"

This was Jacques' suggestion, not mine. He's always wanting to improve his English and insists we only speak French around others.

His grin is wicked as he comes around the bed and wraps his arms around my waist, "*Tu aimes quand je parle français.*"

I like it when he speaks French? Well, yes, yes, I do. "Stop using my weakness against me." I wrap my arms around his neck and meet his lips halfway.

He pulls me flush against him, deepening the kiss as the intercom buzzes from the kitchen. We pull away with a groan.

"Are you expecting anyone?" I step back and head to the kitchen.

"Not yet," Jacques says behind me. "Claude and Penny are not due to pick us up for another hour."

Claude, Penny, and their two children, Amélie and Henri, are on the same flight as us so we're carpooling to the airport. We'll travel to Melbourne together and then part ways. They'll go to Adelaide to visit Penny's family while Jacques and I fly north to Surfers Paradise.

I stride to the kitchen and tap the screen to view the video. Then gasp.

"No. Way," I whisper.

"Jane?" Jacques calls. "Who is it?"

No, no, no. I can't face her. Not today. Not ever.

My heart pounds and the hairs on the back of my neck stand on end. Fight or flight kicks in and I hightail it back to the bedroom, straight for Jacques' walk-in wardrobe and hide amongst his suits.

"Jane?" Jacques comes in and pulls the suits apart, his brow creased in confusion. "What *are* you doing?"

"It's your *Mum*," I whisper, pointing in the direction of the kitchen.

"Maman?" His eyebrows shoot up. "Here?"

I nod, swallowing the lump in my throat, and my arm falls to my side. Jacques goes to answer the intercom.

I feel like a right ol' fool, hiding in amongst Jacques' suits—how did I not know he had so *many*? —but I'm not ready to face Angélique DuPont. I still have nightmares from the last time. That's why I ran back to Australia without Jacques.

Does she have a sixth sense or something? Does she know we're flying home today?

In a matter of minutes, voices filter through to the wardrobe and my skin prickles when I recognise Angélique's. They're not talking loud but it's still unmistakable.

One of the suit jackets tickles my arm and I whack it aside. This is ridiculous. Why am I hiding? I won in the end, didn't I? Jacques chose *me*, not them. I should be stronger now. It's time to prove I'm not afraid of her.

Or at least give the impression I'm not.

So, drawing in a breath, I count to ten before forcing myself out of hiding. On the way to the kitchen, each step is rigid, my breathing laboured. Before I exit, I draw in one more breath and release it slowly as I step through the door, head held high.

Both Jacques and Angélique turn to me. Jacques sends me a tight smile, but Angélique only sticks her nose in the air and ignores me. This is an improvement.

Angélique says something in an urgent tone to Jacques. It's in French, but she's speaking so softly I can't understand her. Jacques responds hotly then storms away, past me, and into the bedroom, closing the door after him. I turn back to Angélique who is hovering in the kitchen.

I grind my teeth as we stare at each other. Any fear I had is gone. She's upset Jacques and that is *not* on. Her cool but intense gaze doesn't have the intended effect. When she glides over to me, still as perfect as ever, I keep my face neutral.

Although when she stops in front of me, she's less than perfect.

Grey hair roots are on display, and with no makeup on, she has heavy bags under her eyes. She looks her sixty-or-so years plus some, with wrinkles etched on her forehead and around her eyes.

Her attire, too, is nothing like the immaculate outfit she wore last time. Today she's wearing a onesie-type thing, but it's old. Faded. Not the latest fashion. I don't think it's *any* fashion.

"*You* are still here," she says in English, in that same regal tone. Her critical gaze rakes over me from head to toe.

Still as intimidating as ever too. Even though I'm properly dressed today, she still has a way of making me feel like I'm half-naked.

"As you can see," I say calmly. "I don't take threats lightly."

She sniffs. "I do not wish to rehash the past. I have a small favour to ask of you."

"Of *me*?" I point at my chest.

She raises one unmanicured eyebrow. "Who else, hmm?" She huffs an impatient sigh. "I do not have time for this. If you care about my son, all I ask is you talk some sense into him. Can you do that?"

Patronising much? Geez. Still, I'm intrigued, and I nod despite myself. Satisfied with this, she gives a single nod, turns, and leaves. I have no idea *what* I'm supposed to be talking sense into him about, but I'm sure he'll tell me.

When the door closes, I take a deep breath and go into our bedroom. Jacques is standing at the window overlooking the city. The sun is shining today, making everything look so bright and alive.

"Hey." I stand beside him. "Sorry I freaked out before."

He gives me a weak smile but says nothing.

I reach for his hand and hold it tight. "Everything okay?"

Jacques squeezes my hand then removes it and runs his hands through his hair, massaging his scalp before crossing his arms across the window and resting his forehead on them.

"Papa is ill," he says at last, his breath fogging up the glass.

Oh. I see. That must've been what they were bickering about.

Let me guess, she wants Jacques to see him, but he said no? Is *that* what she wants me to talk sense into him about? I mean, I suppose I understand. Marcel *is* Jacques' father. But it's not like they've been part of our lives over the past year. There is no recovering from the controlling ways of the DuPont parents, or the emotional abuse they inflicted on their children. Nor is there any overlooking their questionable business practices. I'm not privy to all the details, but Jacques tells me when he takes on new clients that have come over from Entreprises DuPont.

Still, Angélique did ask me to help, so I should try even if I do take Jacques' side. As much as I'm looking forward to going home and seeing my parents again, Jacques comes first in my life now. If I've learnt one thing from being in a long-term relationship, it's that it's all about giving and taking equally. No matter how much *I* might want to return, this must take precedence.

"I'm so sorry, Jack." I rest a hand on his back. "Is it serious? We can always postpone our trip and visit your dad."

There, I've done as she asked. Is it talking sense into him? Maybe not, but I'm also not going to force him into doing something he doesn't want to do. He's a grown man who can make his own decisions.

Jacques shakes himself and he stands up straight, turning to me. His usually vibrant, brown eyes are dull and glazed over. Just goes to show, no matter how estranged you may be from your family, this sort of news is crippling.

"Maman did not say how serious it was, just that he is ill and I should see him." His face darkens. "I owe him nothing. I am sure he will recover soon and she is worried about nothing." He draws in a deep breath, releasing it slowly before taking my hand to hold it between both of his. "No, do not postpone. We will continue as planned." He releases my hand and removes his phone from his pocket, tapping the screen. "We must finish packing."

"Wait." I grab his hand and pull him towards me, wrapping my arms around him. He does the same and we embrace for a few seconds. I'm reminded once again how much I love him, and how my life will never be the same without him. He's completed me in so many ways and is my forever man.

I step out of his embrace but keep hold of his hands. "Anything I can do to help, I'm here. You know that, right?"

His smile comes easier this time, and he leans in to press his lips against mine, never failing to prove his love with one simple kiss.

"Thank you, Jane."

⤜⤛⤛

Over thirty hours later, with two stopovers, and little sleep, we finally make our descent into the Gold Coast. My heart leaps and excitement skirts along my skin. I confirm everything is set for landing, then turn to the window and glance out, only to be met with raindrops on the glass and thick cloud cover.

The plane jumps as it soars through the clouds and comes out beneath them. The view never fails to take my breath away—tall beachside accommodation lining the foreshore, a stretch of white sand below it, and the grey, violent ocean with frothy waves crashing on the shore. I haven't once regretted leaving Adelaide to move here.

Nothing can douse my excitement as I turn to Jacques sitting in the aisle seat, and exclaim, "We're home!"

He removes his earbuds and glances out the window over my shoulder. "It is raining, not the return you wanted." He smiles at me, but it's forced.

He hasn't been the same since Angélique's visit. It must've been a shock to see her. I just don't fully understand the point of it. If she didn't say how ill Marcel was, which to me implies he can't be *that* ill, what was the point of her visit?

I shrug and try to keep my tone light-hearted. "I don't care, I'm just happy to be back."

The next few minutes are a blur as we go through the process of landing, disembarking, picking up our luggage, and going through security and passport control. The excitement from being home has passed and jetlag has set in. My feet and legs are heavy. My brain is in a fog. I need sleep and lots of it.

Once outside, Jacques requests an Uber and we stand at the waiting bay. It's eight a.m. and already humid because of the rain. A trickle of sweat slides down my back.

The Uber arrives a few minutes later, and we slide into the backseat. Tiredness catches up with me and I yawn, resting my head on Jacques' shoulder.

I groan when he moves his shoulder and I lift my head, scowling at him.

"No sleeping, remember?" He says with a smile. "We agreed to stay awake."

Ugh. I groan again and scrub my hands over my face. Jetlag is a bitch. Jacques is right, staying awake is the best approach to getting over it quicker.

"Will your parents be at our apartment?" Jacques presses the button to lower the window a crack.

I nod and blink a few times to keep my eyes from closing. "I gave them the code to the key safe. They should have arrived last night."

Jacques nods and turns to glance out the window at the buildings, cars, and pedestrians speeding by. "Good, I am looking forward to seeing them."

His shoulders are tense and my heart breaks for him. Gosh, how could I forget? The moment Mum and Dad met Jacques in person, they fell in love with him. Treated him like the son they never had.

They've been more like a family to him than his own. Is that why he didn't want to postpone our trip?

Now it all makes sense, why he's been so quiet. He probably feels guilty that he'd rather come to Australia to see *my* parents.

Jacques and I are taking a month off before I search for another job, and he goes back to work. One of those weeks will be with Mum and Dad, and they'll be staying with us. They offered to pick us up from the airport, but because our flight was early, I told them we'd find our own way home.

Turning to glance out the window, I watch the dark blue ocean speed by, still in awe at how much my life has changed. Who would've thought I'd go to Paris, meet a rich guy, and have a long-term relationship with said rich guy? Not me! The biggest challenge of this new life is staying grounded. I don't ever want to forget who I am—the girl who emphathises with those in need. Being in a relationship with someone who has money is a real eye-opener. It's so *easy* to get anything I want, but I can't let money blind me. I don't ever want to stop caring.

I blink when the Uber stops in the circular driveway of the sky-scraper apartment building. Jacques and I climb out as the driver places our luggage on the path in front of the entryway. With a wave, he gets in the car and drives away. A middle-aged male porter comes out with a trolley, greeting us with a single nod.

I wave at him with a bright smile, remembering him from our last stay.

"Good morning, Mr DuPont, Ms Collins." He starts loading our luggage onto a trolley. "Welcome home."

"*Merci,*" Jacques says, distracted while he unlocks his phone.

It's odd, I've always noticed he tends to slip more French words in around people he doesn't know well.

With the trolley loaded, the porter tips his cap, turns, and makes his way back into the building.

I turn back to Jacques and rest a tentative hand on his arm. "You okay?"

His head jerks up and he blinks a couple of times. "I received an email from Rémy."

"Your brother?"

Jacques nods but locks the phone and pockets it. "Nothing important." He takes my hand and flashes me a too-bright smile. "Let us go up and see your parents. I would like to forget about life in Paris for a short while. This is our time now."

Together we go inside and to the bank of elevators, my mind going over everything that has happened. A troubling, unsettling feeling lodges itself deep in my gut.

First Angélique and now Rémy.

Why do I get the feeling Marcel isn't just 'ill'?

Chapter 2

Jacques

I stand in front of the floor-to-ceiling window, admiring the kilometres of white sand and dark blue ocean. In my periphery, I am aware of the city skyline, but the ocean commands my full attention. The rain stopped an hour ago and the clouds have cleared. It is as though it never rained.

This is a view I will never tire of. The moment I arrived in Surfers Paradise with Jane one year ago, this became my new home. The humidity is taking a lot of getting used to, and I am far from acclimatised, but I love my life in this beautiful city. I will endure the weather for as long as I must if it means having this life.

Paris is in my blood, but for the first time ever, I have a real home. Jane and I chose this apartment together with no influence from anyone. We bickered about the rent amount until we agreed on a budget. When we went shopping for items we needed, we bickered over the cost of those too.

Jane's laughter rings out from the kitchen where she is with her parents. It washes over me like a balm and I smile. Every day I am so thankful to have her in my life.

I do not mean for us to bicker over silly things like the quality or cost of items. It appears wanting the best of everything is also in my blood. I know it frustrates Jane that I do not always consider all options.

I am learning, but it takes time.

I always thought I was frugal and compared to my family I am. Smart investing is one thing, but buying the highest quality of everything is not always necessary. In an economy where inflation is happening before our eyes, we must be careful.

The success of Solutions Exécutives has stabilised my financial status, but I am aware it can change unexpectedly. I do not want to get so comfortable that I risk losing everything over a stupid decision.

Turning away from the window, I go over to the bed where my suitcase is. I must hurry so I can join Jane and her parents. I told her I would be with them soon, but I needed a few moments to myself. My mind is still going over the fact that Papa is unwell. Maman was evasive and would not reveal the extent of his illness, only suggesting I see him but not going into detail. But she was not herself. She looked unkempt. I have never seen her in that state. I can only assume it is nothing but another attempt at manipulation.

Still, I am unsure if I made the right decision in leaving. I was desperate to return to Australia, and not at all ready to face my family. They have not contacted me for over one year. Why should I drop everything for them now?

Then I received Rémy's cryptic email, also suggesting I come home but not revealing why.

I am not playing their games. Not again. If Papa really is ill, they must tell me what is wrong.

Unzipping my suitcase, I flip the lid back. Every movement is heavy, jetlag setting into my limbs. I pick up some shirts to put away, realising as I open the drawer that they're not clean. I shake my fuzzy head and sigh. I understand Jane's desire to sleep. The shower I had earlier, and fresh clothes, have helped a little, but I need a long sleep.

My phone vibrates on the bedside cupboard. Claude is replying to my last message saying they are in Adelaide. He also sends a picture with the four of them looking frazzled and worse for wear after travelling. Penny and Claude have scruffy hair and bags under their eyes. Amélie has her face scrunched in a wail while Henri sleeps in his pram.

I chuckle and take a selfie in front of the window, making sure to capture the buildings, sand, and ocean in one shot. I send it with the message: **this is what child-free life is like.**

Of course, I do not expect life to always be like this.

Placing my phone on the bed, I start unpacking, putting my clothes in neat piles.

Jane and I have talked about marriage, a home, and children. We want the same things, it is all about timing. She loves her life in Australia and has not held back saying how much she would love our permanent lives to be here. I like it too and that is why, while I am here this time, my focus is on finding office space on the Gold Coast. Claude and I talked about expanding overseas and this is the perfect opportunity to do so. Jane is also aware of our plans, but does not know where. I hope to surprise her.

Claude joining my business as a partner has been the best decision. We share an assistant now and are advertising for more positions in Paris, which Claude is overseeing.

Over the last three months, we have had an uptick in clients. Some have come across from Entreprises DuPont with sordid tales of inappropriate, bordering on illegal, contracts. Others who have told us that they did not consider Entreprises DuPont since they heard about their bad business practices.

This is great for us, but now that I am aware Papa is ill, I wonder if he is taking a break from running the business while he recovers. He always managed to keep the dishonest side of their business under wraps. If it is getting out, someone else must be running it, but who?

I shake the thought out of my head. It is of no concern to me.

Jane's voice draws closer then the door bursts open. My heart stutters as she enters with a bright smile. No matter how tired she is, to me she is perfect. Her blonde hair hangs in waves around her shoulders, her skin aglow. She's wearing a white tank top, and denim shorts that show off her long legs and shoeless feet. Queensland agrees with her. Settling here is the best decision.

"Mum's cooking a late breakfast," she says. "Are you hungry?"

A waft of bacon reaches my nose. Olivia Collins, or Liv as she prefers, is an excellent cook. "Starving. I will be out in a few minutes." We ate a small meal on the plane, but the food does not match a homecooked meal, especially Liv's.

Jane blows me a kiss and then closes the door. A silly smile fixes itself on my face as I glance at my phone, finding a reply from Claude.

Jealous. Looking forward to seeing your pad when we visit. Hope you're ready for the invasion.

When Penny and Claude could not make it to Australia for Christmas, we decided to travel together. They are coming to visit us during their last two weeks in Australia. I smile and send a reply.

Looking forward to it.

I finish unpacking then place the empty suitcase under the bed. A few moments later, I enter the open-plan kitchen, dining, and living area where Liv, Jane, and her father William are sitting at the table. The apartment is smaller than mine in Paris, but it is homely. A word I never thought would describe a place of my own.

It is modern looking in white, grey, black, and brown. Jane has added splashes of colour in pillows, photos, paintings, and rugs. Sliding doors open to a balcony overlooking the ocean and the city is to the left. The last time we were here, Jane and I spent many mornings enjoying the sunrise on that balcony.

William grins at me. "Here he is! Come and join us, Jack. I hope you're hungry because Liv's been cooking up a storm."

I love that they call me Jack. It is only them, and Jane, who call me that. I like it. It is special somehow.

Jane rolls her eyes. "Dad, I already asked him that."

"Can't be too sure." William picks up his fork and reaches across to spear a sausage.

I chuckle and go over to sit next to Jane. Plates of hot food are laid out in the centre of the table, and my stomach rumbles in appreciation.

William is a tall, well-built man, his mostly grey hair cropped close to his head, and clean shaven. I do not think I have ever seen him with more than a day's stubble. He is in his early sixties but could pass for early forties. He keeps active in his carpentry business and by jogging daily. When they visit, or we visit them, we jog together each morning. It allows us to bond. He has become the loving father I never had.

"Thank you, Liv, for cooking breakfast." I start piling food onto my plate. Bacon, eggs, sausage, mushrooms, hashbrowns, and fried tomatoes.

"You're welcome." Liv's cheeks turn pink. "I like to be useful."

I can see the resemblances between Jane and Liv. They both have blonde hair, but Liv's is darker and streaked with grey. She has darker blue eyes, and William's are lighter, which explains where Jane got her eye colour.

While we eat breakfast, Jane and I fill them in on the last six months in Paris. William is always interested in my business and has lots of questions. When we finish eating, William and I clean up and stack the dishwasher while Jane helps Liv make coffee.

With mugs in hand, we all go out onto the balcony. It is mid-morning, and the city is alive with people on the beach and roads packed with traffic. It is nice to stop and relax rather than be in the hubbub.

"So, I reckon we should have a barbie tonight," William speaks up after a few minutes of silence. "Down at the pool. Jack and I will cook, won't we?"

I raise my eyebrows at him and he laughs. I laugh too because this has become a thing between us. We see each other two or three times when we are in Australia and having a 'barbie', which I remember Jane telling me is a barbeque, is a regular occurrence. It is always a fun evening and I enjoy standing over the barbeque with William, beer in hand, cooking the sausages, or 'snags', as William calls them.

"A barbie sounds great," I say, and everyone laughs. "What?" I glance around. "I did not say it that badly."

There is a twinkle in Jane's eye as she sits straighter in her chair, clears her throat, and in a stronger Australian accent says, "Your Australian is terrible, mate. You still haven't mastered the accent. You are very French. It's *barbie*."

Liv and William chuckle but they do not understand the inside joke. I laugh and rest my arm across Jane's shoulders, pulling her into my side so I can kiss her temple.

"I will never master your weird accent," Jane says as she snuggles into my side.

"Nor I yours."

She grins at me and we fall into silence and stare out over the ocean, sipping coffee. The breeze is balmy, the fronds of palms along the esplanade swaying majestically. It is peaceful, magical, and I am in the best company.

My phone buzzes in my shorts pocket and I take it out. Jane moves away and slides down in her chair, stretching her long legs to catch the morning sun. Another message from Claude flashes up on the screen with a link to a news article. I tap on it and a page opens to a reputable news website in Paris.

The headline '*Entreprises DuPont: Rémy DuPont steps in as CEO, fears for Marcel's health*' stares back at me and my heart stutters to a stop. Well. It answers my suspicions about the company not doing well. Rémy is a terrible businessman, and he is probably unaware of the terrible business practices.

It does not answer how bad Papa's health is because the media can never be trusted to provide factual information.

Another message comes through from Claude.

Did you hear about this? Do you know what's going on?

I type back what little I know, then tell him to enjoy his holiday and we will discuss it when he visits. It will give me time to read the article too.

Pocketing my phone, I stare out over the ocean again and try to relax but I cannot switch off. The euphoria of being back, the bright future I have planned for Jane and me, is tainted. In the space of a few hours, everything is different. I do not need this uncertainty.

I will reply to Rémy's email and ask for information. Until I know what is going on and how bad Papa is, I will not do anything.

I am not going to lose the future I have planned for Jane and me.

Chapter 3

Jane

S itting on the edge of the lagoon pool, my feet dangle in the water. It's cool after the sticky and humid day we've had. No, that should be *days*. It's been like this since we got home four days ago. It's summer, and it's Queensland, this is normal, but geez give me dry heat any day.

It's five p.m. and the humidity is still thick in the air, weighing heavy like a blanket. Sweat drips down my back and soaks into the band of my bikini bottoms.

When I haven't been taking Mum and Dad sightseeing, I've been living in the lagoon pool. It's great to stop and relax, rather than always being busy with life and work. I can enjoy the resort where we live. Yes, that's right, we live in a *resort*. Two years ago, I would never have thought I'd be here. It's such a different world. A paradise.

The apartment complex has a leisure area with a manmade lagoon pool and sandy beaches, a spa at one end, encompassed by sub-tropical gardens and lounge chairs. There are barbeque facilities a few metres away with two barbeques, one on either side. It's first in, first serve every day. Behind a bamboo fenced-off area is a garden and more lounge chairs for those who want to tan rather than swim.

Moving my feet, the water ripples around my legs. The sun moves between two fronds of a palm tree, its rays shining right into my eyes. Squinting, I turn my head away, spotting Jacques crossing the bridge from the apartment complex across the pool towards me. He's in swimming shorts only, his tanned, toned chest on display, the late afternoon sun making the sheen of sweat shimmer. He was so pale when he first came to Australia, but he tans well. Like *insanely*, beautifully well.

Unlike me who still burns, which means my skin never tans. *Ugh.*

I slip into the lukewarm water to move away from the bright sun, leaning against the tiles of the pool. The last few days with Mum and Dad have been lovely and I love seeing Jacques comfortable around them. Relaxed and natural.

Except...

He hasn't *been* here. Physically, yes, but not mentally. I understand the situation with Marcel and the rest of his family must be troubling him and not being in Paris would make it even worse. He emailed Rémy but last I heard he hadn't replied. I don't understand that family. How hard is it to give an update on someone's health? What's the point of keeping it secret?

Should I suggest he go back to Paris? It wouldn't make me a very good girlfriend if I don't. I mean, I don't want him to. This is supposed to be *our* time in Australia. It's selfish, I realise that, but I must think about what's best for him. He may not want to.

I know Jacques pretty well, and he'll be struggling with an internal battle. Wondering how sick Marcel is, or if his family has ulterior motives. After all, Jacques has been removed from the will and disowned by the family, what could they want with him?

Jacques slides into the water and comes around to face me, pulling me flush against his warm, wet skin. His eyes are bright and shining, his shoulders relaxed. He's happy. *Genuinely* happy. I sigh in relief.

"*Bonjour beauté,*" he says with that heart-stopping dimpled smile, then leans in and presses his soft lips against mine.

Such a simple display of affection but my heart races and it's like falling for him all over again. It's these little things I love. Every morning, and every time he greets me, he says the same thing. Ever since the morning he surprised me with breakfast in Paris.

The softness of his lips never fails to set me alight. The strength in his arms as he holds me close, keeping me protected and secure. Oh, how I love this man.

"Well, hello to you." I breathe out a shaky breath when we pull away. "I was wondering where you were."

"I was helping your Papa prepare dinner. He is cooking a barbeque again."

"Dad loves his barbies. It's their last night with us tomorrow night, why don't you cook your ratatouille?"

He makes a *mean* ratatouille. It was the first thing he cooked for me all those months ago.

Jacques' eyes light up but then fade. "He did not seem to like the idea last time I suggested it."

Oh yes, I remember Dad's pale face when Jacques suggested it a couple of nights ago. He's never liked veggies, which always surprises me since he's so fit and healthy. It must be all the salad and fruit he eats instead.

"We'll surprise him," I say matter-of-factly. "He won't know what's hit him until we serve dinner, and he won't be rude enough to not eat it. Dad's a creature of habit, he'll eat the same thing every day. I bet he'll be pleasantly surprised."

The thing with ratatouille, it's not just a plate of bland vegetables. It's such a flavour bomb and if anything can convince Dad to eat veggies again, this will do it.

Jacques is wary but nods. "Okay."

"Come on," I slide out of Jacques' grasp, "let's go for a swim."

I dive under the depths and push against the wall, the water rushing against my ears. When I rise for air, I swim towards the end of the lagoon with long strokes. Within seconds Jacques gains on me and overtakes. He's faster and stronger, but we enjoy swimming together at our own pace.

After a few laps, we stop in the deep end, treading and I'm panting slightly. It's a great workout.

He comes up to me and wraps his arm around my waist as we continue treading, our legs occasionally brushing. He leans in to kiss me softly and slowly, pouring his love into it. When he pulls back, he rests his forehead against mine.

"I am sorry," his warm breath fans my face, "I have not been myself for a few days."

"You're worried about the situation back in Paris?"

His lips purse into a thin line and gives the briefest of nods.

"It's okay to be concerned." My legs are getting tired, so I swim over to the side and pull myself up to sit on the tiled edge.

Jacques joins me, running a hand through his wet hair. "Why should I after everything that has happened?"

There is no mistaking the bitterness in his voice.

"Do you regret how it all ended?" I wait with bated breath while he thinks it over.

"No," he finally answers, "I have you; I could never regret that." His smile is tight, but there is truth in his eyes. "But I am confused. If they did not care about me, what is the point of telling me Papa is ill? Why did they not say how serious it is? It does not make sense. I can only conclude they are playing their usual games and I am not going to let it bother me anymore."

Uncertainties start to creep in. If Marcel really is sick, what will happen? Will we have to go back to Paris? I want to stay here, but whatever happens must be what's best for us. Now isn't the time to overthink this when we know so little.

Shaking the thoughts from my head, I loop my arm through Jacques', squeezing it. "You can't help the way you feel, Jack. Don't be so hard on yourself. If you want to go back to Paris, I'll understand."

Because he may have to, and I'd support that. It would only be temporary.

He jerks upright and turns to me in surprise. "Do you want me to go back?"

I laugh in disbelief. "No, of course not. I only suggested it in case you thought it was a good idea. It'll be easier to get answers if you're there."

He shakes his shoulders, his jaw moving as he grinds his teeth. "Thank you, but no. I will not return."

I nod, relief washing over me.

Changing the subject, I say, "I'm taking Mum to the night markets after dinner, do you want to join us?"

He shakes his head. "No, you go with her. It will be a little while until you see her again." He kisses my cheek and then stands. "I will go and help cook dinner."

⟶⟩⟩⟩ ⟨⟨⟨⟵

The night-time balmy breeze caresses my skin. The air is tinged with meaty, spicy food and mixed with the saltiness of the ocean. The Esplanade is lined with stalls on either side in a variety of colours, decorated with fairy lights. There is so much available to buy—jewellery, art, clothes, bags, hats, hot food, gourmet artisans, fresh produce. The walkway is packed with people, and live music from the other end of the market thrums through the crowd. Everyone is smiling and it's an all-round merry atmosphere.

The produce here is amazing. Jacques and I often come on Saturdays to stock up on local fresh food.

Mum comes to a sudden stop and groans.

"Mum?" I turn in alarm to find her holding onto the pole of a marquee, rubbing her eyes. "What's wrong?"

She glances at me, squinting. "I'm okay, the sun caught my eye that's all." She dismisses it and turns to the stall selling bright beach clothes, searching through them. "What do you think of this?" She holds out an ocean-blue kaftan.

I study her for a moment, but when she appears to be back to normal, I shrug it off and reach out to finger the soft material. "I love it, it'll match your eyes."

While Mum continues sifting through the rack for any other clothes, I cross over to an artisan stall selling cheese that Jacques and I love. I buy some and have a little chat with the girl behind the counter until Mum joins me with her purchases.

We reach the end of the market and turn to head back to the apartment.

"I can't believe you're going home on Friday," I say with a sigh. "I'm going to miss you and Dad."

When Mum stops and takes my hand, I turn to her. Her eyes are watery but she's smiling. "Oh, Jane, we miss you too, but we are so proud of you."

"Yes, Mum." I laugh. "Don't go all mushy on me."

"It's just so good seeing you happy." Mum averts her gaze to look out over the dark ocean. "Have you and Jack decided where you're going to settle yet?"

Ah. *That's* why she's weepy-eyed.

"Not yet, no." I start walking and Mum follows. "I'll tell you once we've decided."

Mum sighs but says nothing. She doesn't need to. She wants us to stay here but she doesn't want to be pushy. Of course, *I'd* love to stay here too, but it's not that simple. There are so many factors involved.

Walking in silence back to the apartment, we pass groups of people on their way to the markets.

We arrive back a couple of minutes later. My phone vibrates as Mum and I stop in front of the elevators. I remove it to see Regina's name on the screen. We send texts to each other sometimes, but I haven't seen her for ages. I think the last time was the day Jacques and I left for the Gold Coast.

I'm moving to the GC! I've got the best job offer for you. Great career opportunities, and we can work together again. Call me tomorrow and I'll fill you in. Reg xx

I swallow the excitement rising within me. A job *here*? Of course, I know nothing about it, but Regina has always been good to work for. This could be perfect. And honestly, I'm so sick of being out of work and flitting from position to position. As much as I love the regular breaks, I can't deny I miss the security of a permanent job. That's been one of the hardest parts of moving between countries, I'm always job searching. I've applied for permanent jobs that promise remote working but when I tell them I'm between countries, they run a mile. What's the point of remote then? Geez.

If Regina insists it's a great job offer, I get the feeling it's going to be hard to resist. This could be problematic. I can't get excited about a job prospect when there's still the chance Paris might be our permanent home.

But I don't want it to be.

Guilt replaces the excitement. It's not all about me, remember? Damn that selfish streak that keeps rearing its ugly head.

Mum peers over my shoulder, reading the message, and she glances at me with a smile. "Oh Jane, how wonderful! Now you have to stay!"

The elevator dings and the doors open. When we step inside, Mum is still grinning, humming to the elevator music, but my heart sinks to my toes as I pocket my phone. I won't bother replying, I'll wait to talk to her tomorrow.

Chapter 4

Jane

The next morning, Jacques says he's going out, but doesn't tell me where. He doesn't need to of course, but it's unusual because we always tell each other where we're going. More for security purposes than anything else. It's weird that he didn't even give me a hint. Usually, he'll say he's popping out, down to the servo or whatever, to grab what he needs.

He doesn't use the words 'popping' or 'servo' though, he's too French for that.

My point is, he's gone out with a fleeting 'see you this afternoon'. No hint. Nothing. What's he up to, I wonder?

With Mum and Dad on a morning river cruise, food and coffee provided, I've got some time alone, which has been bliss.

Dressed in my navy and white bikini with a floral sundress thrown over the top, I grab my tote bag and slip thongs on my feet before leaving. Being within walking distance from the beach is the selling point for me. The pool is great and all, but nothing beats the expanse of the blue ocean.

I slip the tote onto my shoulder, put earbuds into my ears and leave the apartment. Once I'm out of the elevator and on the street, I ring Regina.

"Jane, I'm so glad you called!" She sounds tinny and echoey, I must be on speaker.

"Hey Reg, what's this about you moving to the Gold Coast? I thought you'd never leave Adelaide."

"You made the coast sound so enticing, and there's less of a man drought than in SA, so I figured why the hell not? I'm moving across next week and start my new job the following Monday."

I stop at a road and press the pedestrian button to cross. "That's awesome, I'm happy for you. What's the go with this job offer though?"

"I've been asked to put a team together and I need you on it. The job is everything you do best, Jane. An off-the-shelf program that companies buy and you'll be the one to implement, coordinate, train new users, and manage everything. It's the same as what you did in Paris, but no travelling. You'll work in the office but contact with clients will all be online unless they're local."

The little man turns green, and I cross the road. Regina's description of the job is running around my mind. It's what I want and need.

"Plenty of room for career growth too," Regina adds.

There's the kicker. "Reg, I'm only here for six months. That's the last thing on my mind."

Regina sighs. "Jane, you can't keep putting your career on hold forever. What happened to that ambitious, career-focused girl I sent to Paris?"

Her words catch me off guard.

That girl disappeared in Paris, got caught up in the drama that followed her. By the time I came back to Australia, I was an emotional wreck. A career was the last thing on my mind. Then Jacques followed me here and the rest is history. So caught up in our life together, in adjusting to life in two different countries, a career wasn't important.

Maybe it's time to consider it again.

"I didn't think I was interested in a career anymore, but—"

I bite my tongue. Is *this* particular job the right one?

"But?" Regina coaxes.

"I'd like to think about it again, but is this job the right one?"

"Of course it is! You'll be working with me, we always made a good team, didn't we?"

I smile. "Of course we did." I sigh and step to the side, leaning against the warm bricks of a building. "Truth is, I don't want to live in Paris anymore. I just want to stay here, is that too much to ask?"

My eyes brim with unexpected tears and I blink to hold them back. Where did they come from? I think I'm more homesick than I realised. The thoughts are not new to me, they've been on my mind for a couple of months, but I always vowed I'd never speak them aloud. It feels like a betrayal to Jacques. Paris is the only city he's ever known and I shouldn't dismiss the possibility that *he* may want to stay.

Drawing in a breath to control the sudden influx of emotion, I push off the wall and start walking again.

When Regina says nothing, my anxiety spikes. "I'm a terrible person, aren't I?"

A few metres away, the sun glistens on the water. Palm trees line the esplanade and I pick up my pace, needing to be in the water. The one place that helps me think clearly.

"You're not a terrible person, Jane. I think it's natural to want to stay in one place and make a career. You're an individual with dreams, you shouldn't lose sight of them because of a man. Trust me, they're not worth it."

"Hey, that's not fair. Jack's not to blame in any of this. And he *is* worth it."

I will swear by this to my last dying breath. Jacques has not set one foot wrong. All these feelings are *my* doing, not his. He's always communicated how he feels, it's me, yet again, who hasn't been entirely truthful.

I find it so difficult to tell him how much I *don't* want to live in Paris because I don't want to hurt him. Yes, he's aware I want to settle in one place, but he doesn't realise how deep my feelings run.

Hell, *I* didn't know until I unleashed them on Regina.

Regina huffs on the other end. "Sorry, that was out of line. I'm bitter I suppose. Been single too long." She laughs it off, but it sounds forced. "You've lost your footing a bit, that's all. I can help you. Take the job, Jane."

This is just like when the devil offered Eve the forbidden fruit. Yet it's just a job, right?

"It *is* tempting, but how can I accept a position that means I have to stay here permanently? Everything is still so up in the air about where Jack and I are going to settle."

The words hang in the air as I reach another road. I check both ways for cars then run across when there's a gap.

"What about remote work?" Regina asks as I step onto the sand and find a place to lay out my towel. "If you have to return to Paris, that is. I can trust you to do the job wherever you are."

While her words sink in, I remove my dress and kick my thongs off before settling on the towel. Remote, huh? Perhaps the saying 'it's not what you know, but who you know' is true. I've had no success with remote jobs before now, but Regina is willing to make it happen.

"I appreciate that," I reach into my tote and remove the sunscreen, "so yes of course I'd do it if it came to it." I lather a good amount of cream over my exposed skin, inhaling the scent of coconut it leaves behind.

"So, you'll take the job." Regina asks.

Once I'm lathered, I put the sunscreen away and stretch out my legs. "I'd be crazy not to, so yes I will."

Regina whoops. "You won't regret it! Now, let's talk salary."

We chat a little longer, agree on the salary and a start date, then we hang up. I rip my earbuds out and throw them in my tote bag. I should be elated that I have a job, but I'm still annoyed. At myself, of course.

Jacques has given me the world. Everything I never thought I could have is at my fingertips. I really should appreciate what I have. Why should it matter where I live so long as Jacques and I are together?

Feeling a little less uptight, I get to my feet and run to the water, diving into an oncoming wave. Coming up for air, the coolness of the water and the warm sun on my skin helps me think rationally.

I can't lose control. If I don't want to make the same mistake I did in Paris, I must talk to Jacques about it.

·»»» «««·

Jacques

"Look at the view." I move my phone around to the window overlooking the ocean.

"No one will get any work done," Claude says over the speaker.

"Or they will be inspired to work more," I counter as I move the phone around so Claude can see the rest of the office. We are on FaceTime so I can show him the space I am looking at for the Australian branch.

"I like it," Claude says as Henri starts crying off camera. "A little small though."

I cannot disagree, but I do not think it is so bad for starting up. It has a small kitchenette and two bathrooms. The office space is mostly open plan apart from two smaller offices, one boardroom, and two small meeting rooms.

"Too small, or acceptable to begin with?" I ask.

"Wouldn't it be better to start a little bigger, so we have space to grow? If we start small and grow quickly, we'll have to find another location sooner and it won't be cost effective."

"Hmm." I cannot argue his point. I turn the camera back, so I am looking into it. "I have one more space to visit, then if that is no good, I will have to do some more digging. Can I call you back in half an hour?"

I wince when Henri's cries become ear-piercing.

"Yes, half an hour is fine. I'll try and settle this little guy, too. He's teething again."

"I'm here to help," Penny says off-screen. Seconds later Henri's cries turn into whimpers.

The estate agent comes into the room with a questioning glance, and I hold up one finger. "Claude, I will call you back soon." We hang up and I turn to the agent. "Too small, can I see the next one?"

He nods and taps his iPad a few times. "Of course, Mr DuPont."

The next one is not much better and even smaller. The view is better but that means nothing. The agent and I part ways, with a promise to contact me if he finds anything else.

I had hoped not to work much while Jane and I had this month off, but I must be proactive in finding office space. If something becomes available, I must act fast. But it does not feel like I am working because it is for our future.

I cannot wait to surprise her.

⟫⟫⟩ ⟨⟨⟪

"Jack, you must give me that rata-whatever recipe from last night," William says the next morning when he comes out for breakfast.

I glance at him in surprise the same moment there is a clatter from behind me and a gasp from Liv.

"You what, Dad?" Jane says. "I know you liked it, but you want to make it *again*?"

William slaps my shoulder as he passes, and I grin at him. "I will email it to you." I am happy that I cooked a vegetable dish that William liked.

"Thanks." William joins Jane and Liv at the table, serving himself some breakfast. "I need to make up for it this morning though, double bacon baby." He piles on about twice that much, but no one says anything. "I can get behind rata-thingamy, but I'll never become a vegetarian."

"Ratatouille," Jane and Liv say at the same time.

Chuckling, I turn back to finish making a coffee. I take one over to Liv then come back to start on another.

My phone buzzes on the counter next to me and I pick it up. It is an email...from my sister? What is going on? I have not heard a word from Rémy, so I assumed Papa was fine and they decided not to tell me anymore. Maybe he is not.

I tap open the email and read it.

Dear Jacques,

Maman says you will not see Papa while he is unwell? I wish you would change your mind. It is easier to explain everything in person.

Your sister, Céleste

Brow furrowed and curiosity piqued, I go back to my inbox to re-read Rémy's email.

Jacques,

Why will you not come and see Papa? You must stop this nonsense, we can explain everything when you are here.

Your brother, Rémy

Both emails are almost exact, only altered based on how they are written. Also, Rémy's is in English whereas Céleste's is in French.

This must be some sort of sick conspiracy. I stand by not getting involved in their games. I go back to Céleste's email and type a reply.

Céleste,

I do not understand why I must be in Paris to be told what is wrong with Papa. It is not difficult to tell me over email, but if you refuse to, I will not be returning home.

Jacques

Once sent, I pocket my phone and go back to making coffee. I am not pandering to their needs anymore. Unless there is a valid reason and proof that Papa is very sick, I am not dropping everything like I used to.

Chapter 5

Jacques

"Where are you taking me?" Jane asks.

I hold her hand as I lead her towards the doors of the building. She is blindfolded and her grip tightens when she stumbles on the uneven ground.

"It is a surprise. Now be careful, there are three steps."

I help her up the steps and then lead her through the automatic doors and into the building. A foyer stretches in front of us with elevators at the back, a café in the middle, and a reception and security desk on the right. It is mid-morning and people are milling around talking and laughing as they arrive or leave. Some queue up for coffee, others wait for the next available elevator.

"What's going on?" Jane asks. "It sounds noisy and," she sniffs, "is that coffee? Are we inside a building?" She goes to take the blindfold off with her free hand, but I stop her.

"Trust me," I say as we join a group waiting for an elevator. "We will be there soon. Yes, we are inside, and we are about to go in an elevator."

"Jack, you've got me blindfolded in front of other people?" Jane whisper-yells as we step inside.

One person gives us a curious glance but no one else pays us any attention.

In a louder voice, Jane says, "I know this looks bad, but he hasn't kidnapped me, I promise. This is supposed to be a surprise."

Someone behind us snickers, but no one else says a word and awkwardness settles around us. I should have planned this better. I was so eager to surprise her, all I thought about was getting her here as soon as possible.

Agonisingly slowly, the lift makes its way up multiple storeys, people getting off at different levels. Finally, it reaches the twentieth floor where we are the last two to exit the elevator into an office space. The view is the first thing that catches my eye, on the far wall. It takes my breath away every time. When I showed Claude the space, he joked again that staff would not get their work done, but it is a risk I am willing to take. Happy staff results in positive morale, which means they will be more productive.

The elevator doors slide closed behind us.

"Well, that was awkward," Jane says.

"Sorry." I chuckle. "I did not think it through very well." In hindsight, we could have come after hours, but I wanted Jane to experience the spectacular view in daylight. "Okay, we are here. Are you ready?"

Jane nods.

I step behind her to untie the blindfold.

Before I do, I take a deep, calming breath. I am surprisingly nervous. After all, this is a big deal. I have found the ideal office space.

A small part of me is worried that I have it all wrong. What if Jane would prefer to stay in Paris rather than here?

Deep down I know this is untrue, but the niggle does not go away.

Four days ago, Liv and William flew back to Adelaide. It was Jane's and my first quiet weekend together in a long time, which was bliss. She told me about Regina's call and the job offer. I am happy for her, although I will not lie. I am disappointed. Claude and I discussed having her work at Solutions Exécutives but the timing was never right. At first we had no need for her specific position. The job she did was easily shared between other staff. With the new branch opening though, we would need someone with her skills but Claude and I only agreed on that yesterday. By then it was too late.

Still, I am not *that* disappointed. Nothing can take away the pride I feel at this moment.

Starting my business in Paris and growing it with Claude were proud moments too, but this is bigger somehow.

This time Jane is part of it. While she may not be working for us, she is by my side as it comes together.

I whip the blindfold away and Jane blinks a couple of times, taking in the view first before glancing around the rest of the floor. The space is larger than the others I have seen but still not big enough. There were two floors available for lease, so I leased both. We now have the perfect space to start and grow.

"Um, great view?" Jane's brow creases in confusion. "Nice office, too, but what's it for?"

"Come," I take her hand and lead her over to the reception desk, handing her a manila folder sitting on top.

She takes it from me, her brow furrowed, then opens it and scans the top page. "A lease?" She flicks through the pages then back up at me with an eyebrow cocked. "I don't understand."

Grinning, I open one of the desk drawers and pull out an A4 frame, handing it to her. She takes it from me, studies it, and gasps, her eyes widening.

"A business registration? Executive Solutions?"

I have learned a lot of people here frame the registration of the business name. I thought it was an unusual idea at first, but it grew on me. I completed the registration while we were in Paris and found a frame yesterday. I will hang it on the wall behind the desk.

"Is this what I think it is?" She glances at it again, frowning. "Wait, it can't be, it's not registered to Solutions Exécutives."

Her French is so perfect on those two words, my heart swells with pride.

Her eyebrows knit together. "No, wait, it is. Oh my gosh, Jack! This is the English name!" She puts the frame back on the desk.

"Yes, we are opening our first international office here on the Gold Coast."

"Jack!" She leaps into my arms, wrapping her legs around my waist and her arms around my neck.

I hold onto her, spinning around as she laughs in glee. Her long blonde hair flies out as she throws her head back. When we stop, she grins at me, her eyes shining. If I had any doubt about this decision, this moment confirms it is right.

"Wait." I place her on the ground, and she stares at me, agog. "Does this mean what I think it means?"

The moment I was waiting for. Pulling her flush against me, I capture her gaze. "If you think it means I want us to live in Australia permanently, then yes. If it is what you want too."

"If it's what I want? Does a bear poop in the woods?" She rolls her eyes, but she is grinning.

I stare at her for a long moment. Sometimes she still comes out with odd expressions I do not understand. You would think after one year I would be used to it, but then she comes out with another doozy.

Yes, 'doozy' is a word I have learnt from her. I quite like it.

Jane's laughter rings out, snapping me out of my thoughts. "It's just—"

"An expression, yes I got that. Do you mean it literally?"

"Well, yes but it's an ironic statement. So, you asked if it's what I want so I stated the obvious."

"Ah, I see." I shake my head in amusement. "You still surprise me, Jane Collins. Come on, let me show you around."

Jane's excitement is infectious as I show her around the floor. I tell her about the second floor but do not show her as it is identical. While all the walls have windows, one side is pure glass and that is where the spectacular view is. Three kilometres out of Surfers Paradise, the view is of the cityscape and the ocean beyond.

It is a new and modern office space. The building was only completed in the last few months. Everything inside is new, which means I will not need to plan any renovations. Light and airy, it has a decor of grey with splashes of red, white, and black. Including the standard kitchen, bathrooms, and storage rooms, there is a decent floor area for open plan desks, but also some offices, meeting rooms, and a boardroom.

"I love it," Jane says when we stop at the end of the office. "So, you'll be running it?"

I nod and lean against the windowsill. "Yes, and I will need to put in a few hours of work over the coming days so I can advertise for multiple positions. When Claude and Penny visit, Claude and I will interview suitable candidates." I smile in apology. "I am sorry this is not turning out to be a proper holiday together."

She leans on the ledge next to me, our shoulders touching. "No, but it's worth it, right?"

I nod then push away and stand in front of her, taking her hands. "Claude and I had hoped to offer you a job, but Regina beat us to it."

She bites her lip and smiles guiltily. "I'm sorry. If I'd known what you were planning, I would've told her I was unavailable."

"And missed out on surprising you?"

"Well," she shrugs, "that's a you problem."

We chuckle and I draw her in, kissing her softly. "If it does not work out for Regina, let me know."

"Oh I will." She breathes out, her eyes widening. "Hey, something just occurred to me. I was all ready to work remotely when we returned to Paris if I had to, but now I won't need to!" A slow grin spreads across her face. She shrieks and runs off, spinning, jumping, and exclaiming as she takes everything in again.

There is no way I can remain disappointed when she is this happy. I wanted us to be together in Australia and it is happening. This is enough.

When I reach her at the other end, her cheeks are rosy and she's panting from running. "Jack," she comes up and presses her lips to mine, "I can't tell you how happy I am. Thank you." She frowns. "But your dad, he's still sick."

I grit my teeth and shake my head. "That is of no concern. Neither Céleste nor Rémy have returned my emails. I can do nothing else. I am not putting my life on hold anymore. It is time for us to put our future first."

The shine of happy, unshed tears in Jane's eyes makes my heart warm with delight. Whatever happens, I am determined to put our future first no matter the cost. No one, not even my family, will come between us ever again. I will make sure of it.

Chapter 6

Jane

The early afternoon sun glimmers on the ocean as I sip my cappuccino. There's a lovely cool breeze coming off the water. Large waves are rolling in and crashing on the shore, experienced surfers riding them with a natural flair I can't begin to imagine. They make it appear so easy, but it's not. I've learnt from embarrassing firsthand experience.

For as long as I can remember, I've had surfing on my bucket list. The moment we settled here, I booked my very first lesson. I begged Jacques to join me, but he wasn't interested so he watched. And laughed. And laughed some more, as I tried and failed to stay on the surfboard.

I swear to this day those waves had it in for me. They were trying to *kill* me. Jacques will say I was exaggerating, but I know the truth. The instructor was probably glad to wave goodbye to me. Surfie Jane Collins will never be a thing. But I got to cross an item off my bucket list and a vow to never surf again. For my integrity if nothing else.

The esplanade is jam-packed with people enjoying the sunshine and cooler breeze. Workers on lunch break, some walking and eating, others jogging, others taking their lunch back to the office. Those who aren't working, idle along at their own pace with coffee or food in hand. Some are walking their dogs. Today is a perfect reminder of why I love the Gold Coast so much. And this is my life now. *For good.*

My heart skips as I remember Jacques' surprise a few days ago. I cannot be happier, yet there's still guilt weighing on me after my little whinge to Regina. Because Jacques has given so much up for me and continues to do so, yet I was complaining about not wanting to live in Paris anymore. And now Jacques has given me what I want. I feel guilty because at that moment I didn't think of Jacques. Only myself.

Without my knowledge, he was thinking of me, of *our*, future. Doing everything in his power to find office space so we can start our lives in Australia.

Gosh, I can be such a stupid, selfish fool sometimes.

It's a big lesson learned. To appreciate what I have and what Jacques has given up for me. I mean, what if he doesn't like it here? What if he hasn't told me because he's aware of how much I love it? He may never tell me, but it's a possibility.

I shiver and avert my gaze, finishing my cappuccino. Yes, it's one hell of a reality check.

"I made it! Sorry I'm late."

Starting in surprise, I whip my head up to find Regina standing beside the table, grinning.

"Reg, hi!" I leap out of my chair and embrace her.

She arrived in Queensland yesterday and starts her new job on Monday. She wanted to catch up today before going to the office to meet some of the other staff and sort out the paperwork.

"It's so good to see you!" I step back. "You look *amazing.*"

And she does. Already she fits in. She's dressed in a long summery maxi dress and sandals, her red hair falling in waves around her shoulders, and beach-style jewellery. To my surprise, she's not wearing her usual perfectly applied makeup either. She is *au naturel* and killing it.

"Do I belong?" She places her hands on her hips and poses.

"Totally." I gesture to the spare seat and we both sit. "Do you want anything?"

Regina picks up the menu and peruses it. "I'd love something to eat, I'm famished. What's the food like?"

"Excellent. This is a regular haunt Jack and I come to."

Regina's smile is tight, but I think nothing of it.

"Brill." She gestures for a waiter.

After we've placed our orders, she turns to glance out over the ocean and sighs.

"What a fabulous view," she breathes.

"It's stunning, isn't it? The waves are perfect today."

Regina's laugh is seductive. "I'm not talking about the waves, darling. Mmmhmm, I can get used to this."

Raising an eyebrow, I scan the crowded oceanfront, spotting a man coming out of the waves, a surfboard under his arm. Aged in his early to mid-forties, similar age to Regina, I can't deny he's hot. He's tanned and glistening, with ripped abs, and muscled arms and legs. He runs a hand through his soaked hair, his biceps flexing, while he grins at the women ogling him as they pass.

"Of course, you're not here for the Queensland beauty," I say dryly.

"Oh, I am, just not the natural beauty."

Regina surprises me by standing and ripping off her dress. I gasp and hold my arms in front of my face when I notice she has a bikini underneath. Because *of course* she has. We hadn't agreed to go swimming, she had this *all* planned.

She runs her fingers through her hair, adjusts the bra of her bikini, and then grins. "Excuse me, I'll be right back."

Open-mouthed, I stare after her as she strides in the direction of surfboard-guy. Holy hell, this is a brand new side of Regina. And, *wow*, she's tall with an hourglass figure and legs that go on forever. Since she's the type to wear oversized clothes, for comfort she says, it means I've never taken any notice of her figure. But she is stunning. For her mid-forties, she could pass for someone in her early thirties.

I can't tear my eyes away as she strides up to surfboard-guy and strikes up a conversation, shamelessly flirting. He appears to enjoy the attention, flirting back, and ignoring anyone else. I must give Regina credit, she could pick up any man she wants with her confidence.

Shaking my head, I turn away and check my phone to find a message from Jacques.

Job advertisements are live.

I grin and send back an excited emoji. Over the last few days, I've helped him with the applications for the positions he needs to advertise for. He and Claude came up with the required positions, and I assisted with the wording. Jacques' written English still needs work, so I'm happy to help.

Putting my phone away, I spot Regina walking back with a purposeful swing to her hips. Surfboard-guy is watching with a dumbstruck expression.

"Piece of cake." She grins as she dons her dress and sits down, throwing her hair over her shoulder.

The young waiter returns with our meals and places them in front of us.

"Thanks," Regina glances at his badge and back at him, fluttering her eyelashes, "Tom."

His cheeks turn a bright pink, and he speeds off, tripping over his feet in the process.

I shake my head. "You're something else, Reg. He's half your age!"

"I don't mind being a cougar." She laughs. "But you're right. He is a little too young. As for Vince..." She makes a growling sound and I stare at her.

"Calm down, tiger," I say uncomfortably. "I assume Vince is the guy you cornered on the beach?"

"Yep. We're having dinner tonight and if all goes well, dessert in my hotel room later." She waggles her eyebrows.

"Geez, you're on the warpath."

"Don't I know it? Been too long and I'm done with waiting. I'm *desperate* for a shag. The man drought has been going on for too long."

"Just be careful, Reg." I frown and pick up my cutlery.

She laughs it off and sips her flat white. "I'm a grown woman, Jane, I know what I'm doing."

The aroma of salmon, broccolini, baby potatoes, and hollandaise sauce makes my mouth water. "Of course, but I wouldn't be a good friend if I didn't say it."

Regina stares at me for a long moment. "I appreciate it, Jane, thank you."

She picks up her knife and fork and digs into her meal. I do the same and we talk while we eat. The waves on the shore, the din of cutlery on plates, and the chatter of people soothe me and I feel a little less bewildered.

Social Regina is so different from boss Regina. It's funny, we became friends but didn't socialise outside of work often. Sometimes we'd have drinks after work, or staff lunches, but that was it. When we met up before I moved here, Jacques was with me, so Regina was how I'd always known her.

This new side of her has thrown me.

When we finish eating, we make our way to the office where we'll both be working. It's close so we stroll there, chatting and enjoying the beautiful day.

"Have you met any other staff yet?" I ask as we approach the automatic doors to the high-rise building.

"Only over Zoom." Regina breezes through the doors with me following. "Have you researched the company?"

"Afraid not, I've been too busy enjoying my holidays."

Regina sends me a sharp glare and I grin at her.

"Holidays or not, we want to make a positive impression," Regina says. "I sent you all the information."

"I know you did, but as I said, I'm on holiday. I'll read up before I start."

Regina huffs and stops outside the elevators. "They're a company that designs and sells software. They're starting a new project and I'm forming a team who'll implement and manage it once a client buys the program. Think support team but we don't fix anything. You'll be the one who assists with installation, setup, training, handling technical enquiries, and sending bug tickets to the development team. I do managerial stuff." She waves this off like it's nothing.

Then again, Regina's a natural manager.

I nod and enter an elevator when one opens. At least this time I'm not blindfolded. This makes me smile and it turns into a grin as I remember, yet again, that we're here to stay. Every time I think about it, a thrill shoots right to my toes. I've seen the office space. The business registration. The lease agreement. This is happening!

"What are you grinning about?" Regina asks.

"Just thinking back on when Jack showed me the space he's leased for his Australian office."

I'd texted Regina the same day after Jacques and I left the office.

Regina snorts. "It's about bloody time. Why didn't he sacrifice everything for you straight away?"

"Reg," I hiss, jabbing her in the ribs, "will you stop? I have no idea why you're being like this, but we both agreed, it wasn't one-sided."

Regina purses her lips but says nothing else. I shuffle from foot to foot and let it slide, but it niggles at me.

Why is this bothering her so much, so suddenly?

⇥⇥⟩ ⟨⇤⇤

When I'm done at the office, Regina and I part ways. All the paperwork is done, and we've met the rest of the staff. It's safe to say I think I'm going to enjoy working there. Everyone is easy-going and laid back, just as I like it. On first impressions, no Francine types. Although, I haven't met anyone else from the team Regina is forming. They're all starting at the same time I do.

On the way back home, the cool breeze has gone and the humidity is on the rise. I can't wait to take a dip in the pool later.

When I reach the apartment building, I take the elevator up to our floor, humming a song I heard earlier. My only thought is getting into my swimmers and going down to the pool. I might drag Jacques along if he's not busy.

As I turn the corner to our apartment, I stop humming when I hear a noise. I'm not sure what it is at first, so I wait for it. Then it happens again. Meowing. A cat? I glance up and down the hallway. Nothing. Our door is at the end and there are two others along the wall. Backtracking, I glance down a hallway I bypassed, spotting a little kitten outside, pawing at a closed door. It's a couple of months old.

"Oh, hey kitty." I approach tentatively and kneel beside it. The kitten scuttles back a little, its fur fluffing up, but stops and stares at me, its green eyes wide. It meows again.

From behind the door comes another muffled meow. The mother cat?

"Were you locked out?" I ask the kitten, even though it can't understand me.

It meows again and starts purring. Hey, maybe it can!

It comes over to me and I fall in love with it. It's black with white paws, a white V on its chest and a white moustache. I gave up on the idea of the spinster crazy cat lady life when Jacques came to Australia, but that doesn't mean I don't want a pet cat. I do!

The question is, will Jacques want one? Does he like cats? We've talked about everything from where we'll live, to marriage, to children. But cats? Pets in general? Nope, not once.

Scooping the kitten into my hands, I cradle it in one arm, get to my feet and knock on the door. The muffled meow sounds again but no one answers. They must be out. Not wanting to leave the kitten in the hallway, I take it back to my apartment to keep it safe. I'll come back later.

As I make my way back, the kitten's purring vibrates against my fingers, I tell myself not to get attached. It's likely I won't be able to keep it. I mean, it has a home. Yet, as I unlock the door and step inside, Jacques turns to me with a smile and there's no stopping my next words.

"Can we keep it?"

Chapter 7

Jacques

Sharp claws dig into my calf, and I curse in French. Jane thinks I do not talk in French often while I am in Australia, but if I am alone, or talking to anyone in Paris, I do. Sometimes I need a break from English. It is a difficult language to grasp, and it can be exhausting having to translate words in my head before I say them.

The claws dig into my leg again, but this time closer to my knee. I glance down and see a small black and white figure climbing up my trouser leg and onto my lap. The still unnamed kitten blinks up at me and meows before making short work of climbing onto my shoulder. He settles into a loaf position, purring next to my ear.

I have never had a pet before, so this is new territory for me, but he is very entertaining. I scratch the top of his head and he makes a mewling noise before rubbing his head against my ear. He settles down by laying his small body over my shoulder and resting his head on his two front paws.

The owner of the stray kitten was looking for homes for this one and four others. When Jane found him, he had accidentally been locked out. Must have escaped without the owner's knowledge when they went out. Now he is ours. I was unsure when Jane asked to keep him, but now I am glad I agreed. Our little family is growing.

Turning back to my laptop, I open my email and see more applications for the jobs I advertised last week. They will be running for one more week, but I have already organised interviews for standout applications.

Last night Claude and Penny arrived. They will be staying with us for two weeks before returning to Paris. Claude and I are planning to interview all potential candidates and have job offers sent before they go home. Tomorrow is Monday and we will start the interviews then.

"Any more applications?"

I glance up at the doorway where a dishevelled Claude stands in his pyjamas. He's bleary-eyed from sleep, hair stuck up in all directions.

Claude's voice startles the kitten and he jumps to his feet on my shoulder. I move my head, but the movement startles him again. He rears up, hackles on his back raised, tail fluffed up, two paws upright ready for attack. One paw whacks me a couple of times then he dashes off, down my chest and leg and out of the room.

Claude and I share a surprised glance and we chuckle.

"Yes," I answer his question and beckon him over.

He drags a chair across and together we go through the latest applications, making notes of those I will call tomorrow for interviews.

When we are done, I close the laptop lid. This is all we need to do today. "Coffee?"

Claude shakes his head but does not meet my gaze. "Not yet, thanks." He flicks his gaze up once then drops it again and rakes a hand through his hair. "Jacques, I need to show you something."

He is wearing a serious expression, which is never a good sign. He wore it a lot when he was still working for Maître Tech. Since we became partners, I have not seen it once.

My stomach twists. "What is it?"

"Do you remember that news article I sent you a couple of weeks ago? About your family?"

"Yes, but I forgot to read it."

Claude's smile is tight. "I thought so." He clears his throat. "I need you to read it."

He places his phone on the desk and swipes the screen. After tapping a couple of times, he hands his phone to me.

With a sigh, I take it and reread the headline I remember: *Entreprises DuPont: Rémy DuPont steps in as CEO, fears for Marcel's health*. The article is short and does not say a lot, it is speculation after noticing Papa's absence. The only confirmed fact is that Rémy is acting as CEO.

"Okay." I hand the phone back. "It is nothing earth-shattering. I still know nothing about Papa's health. I emailed both Rémy and Céleste asking for more information, but they are not responding."

"This isn't all though," Claude confesses. "The media has blown up in Paris in the last week. Every day something else pops up about your family."

I shuffle in my seat. "It does not affect me anymore. What happens to them—"

"Also affects you and the Solutions Exécutives name," Claude finishes.

"How? I am keeping my company separate, it has no affiliation with Entreprises DuPont at all. We are competition."

"I hate to break it to you, Jacques, but you will always be a DuPont. If Entreprises DuPont is getting a bad rap, it will reflect badly on our company too. Your name is popping up more in the media, people are asking questions about your whereabouts and why you are not stepping up instead of Rémy. You are the oldest, after all."

Claude taps on his phone and hands it back to me. An article is open with the heading *Where is Jacques DuPont?*

I shudder and look at Claude, my breath catching in my throat. He only nods once, his mouth set in a straight line. Sitting upright in my chair, my heart skips a beat. It has been a long time since my name has appeared in the media as a focus piece. I have always tried to keep a low profile. Moving to Australia seemed like a great way to slip under the radar.

I was wrong.

The people in Paris have not forgotten who I am...a DuPont first and foremost. They assume that Entreprises DuPont will be run by the oldest child if Papa ever retired, or in this case, got sick.

Taking a deep breath, I force myself to read the article.

It is a smear campaign, written to drag my name through the mud; publishing untruths about my character and invalid assumptions about why I am not there. Nothing about Papa's questionable business tactics, or the fact that Entreprises DuPont is sinking.

"*Merde,*"

I mutter, dropping the phone onto the desk.

The article is unpleasant, but I would be happy to shrug it off and ignore it. The only reason I do not is what Claude has already said, and he is correct. We have both worked so hard to make our partnership a success, and articles like this can be devastating.

I glance at Claude sharply. "You did not show me this sooner, why?"

"Would you have read it?" he counters, deadpan.

I rake a hand through my hair. He is right. Again. I did my duty by replying to my siblings and asking for more information, but I have not gone out of my way to find out more. I have not cared enough to do so.

If Claude is the one telling me I must care, it is serious.

"There are many articles, but not all of them are this bad," Claude says. "Although, you might appreciate this one."

He brings it up on his phone and pushes it towards me. Sighing, I read the article painting Rémy in a shining light, making him out to be the golden child who steps in when he's needed most. The one who will move the company forward.

I laugh out loud when I read this and glance up at Claude who is smiling and shaking his head. He is aware, as well as I am, that Rémy does not have the skills to run a successful business.

When I finish reading, I hand the phone back to Claude and run my hands down my face. "What do we do?"

"Conduct damage control." Claude pockets his phone. "First thing you need to do today is write a statement. I'll email it to my trusted journalist contact in Paris. You need to show you're not like your family. Talk about your life in Australia, your growing company, and how you're doing things differently. Solutions Exécutives is getting more exposure, we're building a good name, but a single bad rap can ruin it all. They need a face, *your* face. *Trust.*"

I nod absentmindedly, already thinking about what I will say. So much for not doing anything else work-related today. Claude is right though. This takes priority. I have left too much to him and while he has handled it well, it has not reflected well on me. The whole point of me going out on my own was to prove myself as different to my family. Instead, I have done the opposite.

Perhaps not caring enough about what is going on with my family was a bad idea. Having them cut me off is one thing but ignoring them and not paying attention to what was happening to the DuPont name was wrong. I sometimes forget I cannot escape who I am.

"Jacques," Claude says, his tone light, "your Papa is really sick."

I shudder at his words. *Really sick.* It is the first time someone has not been evasive about it.

"How do you know? I thought it was some big secret. Maman would not tell me in person, Rémy and Céleste refuse to mention it in email." I shrug in defeat.

"Didn't you ever think that maybe they didn't want the media to find out? You've seen the articles already *without* the knowledge."

I stare at him hard, guilt forming deep inside. "No, I did not."

This *does* make sense for why my siblings would not tell me. It does not make sense why Maman did not say anything in my apartment.

"I thought they were playing games or trying to manipulate me to go back home."

Claude smiles sadly. "For once, they weren't. That journalist contact I told you about, I got him to do some digging. He found out everything. I received an email overnight."

I have to admit I enjoyed not knowing, but I cannot avoid it any longer. "What is wrong then?"

Claude hesitates for a second. "It's cancer, Jack. Terminal cancer. He has weeks left at most."

I turn cold. The evasiveness from my family made me think it was something small he would recover from. I did not once think it would be terminal.

"Oh," is all I manage.

Unexpected sadness washes over me, the news hitting me harder than I expect.

"I assume it won't be long until the media knows," Claude says then looks at me for a long moment. "I think you should see him."

There is so much to take in and all I can focus on is the last sentence. I turn my gaze back to him. "What is the point? He has not asked to see me, why should I bother?"

"He didn't but your Maman did, so did Rémy and Céleste. You'll regret it if you don't do this, Jacques."

I turn away and glance out the large window overlooking Surfers Paradise and the ocean beyond. Dark clouds have rolled in over the morning, threatening rain and possibly a storm. The humidity will be very high which confirms my resolve to stay indoors today, maybe go out to the pool later if it is not stormy.

"Jacques."

I blink away my thoughts, recalling what Claude said. Will I regret it? Quite possibly. It will mean going back to Paris, which I did not wish to do, but it would not be for long.

"Maybe you are right," I say. "I will make a plan."

The door bursts open and Jane waltzes in. She is a welcome distraction. Her hair is pulled back and she is wearing a pretty, knee-length summer dress.

"Brekky?" She sends a bright smile to me and Claude.

"Yes please," Claude stands, grips my shoulder in a show of solidarity then walks out.

I can hear Penny with Amélie and Henri. The smell of pancakes makes my stomach rumble.

When the door clicks closed, Jane comes up to me. "You okay?"

I envelop her in my arms and hold her against me, pressing my lips to the top of her head. Her flowery scent is enough to revitalise me and remind me that my life is here. And if I want this, I must visit Papa and put an end to that part of my life once and for all.

"I am now." We step apart and I fill her in on Papa's condition.

She steps back, her eyes shimmering with unshed tears. Despite how they have treated her, and what she knows about them, she is still empathetic.

"Jack, I'm so sorry. Are you okay?"

I shrug. "I feel odd. Sad, I guess, but I do not think he deserves my sadness."

"Hey," she takes my hand and entwines our fingers, "despite everything he's still your father. Being sad is normal." She pauses. "Do you have to go back to Paris?"

"Yes."

Her face drops for a split second but she quickly recovers and nods in understanding.

I squeeze her hand, knowing how much this pains her. We are finding our feet and making big plans. Now this.

"It will not be for long," I console. "I have been cut from the family and the will, what reason do I have to stay for too long?"

Relief fills her eyes, and she nods.

"You will care for the kitten, yes?"

"Of course, and Moe is his name." As if on cue, the kitten comes skidding to a halt at her feet and she bends down to pick him up. She holds him up and points to his moustache. "It suits him, right?"

I chuckle and scratch Moe under the chin. "Yes, it is a good choice." When her smile slips into a frown, I add, "This is just a small hurdle. We will get through this."

She blinks and wraps her free arm around my neck, hugging me close. "I know."

As she says the words, I get this unsettling feeling in the pit of my stomach.

I do not trust my family.

Chapter 8

Jane

Moe is curled up on my lap as I sit on the balcony with a cider. I pat him while sipping from the bottle and staring out over the city and ocean. The balmy breeze caresses my skin and catches on my hair. The waves lapping the shore are gentle. It's soothing, just what I need.

Sometimes when it's rough, my thoughts tumble along with the waves. Today I need my thoughts to be calm. It's been a week since Penny and Claude arrived. I've loved spending time with them, but I've had little time to accept the fact that Jacques must go back to Paris.

Placing my bottle on the small table between the two wicker chairs, I draw in a breath and release it slowly. With the sun behind the apartment building, shadows stretch across the ground and the sky begins to darken. I'm so blessed to have the life I have and I can only thank Jacques for it. He loves it too, and it sucks he must go back. If I ever have to leave, it will be so difficult.

Hell, I don't want to.

Picking up my bottle again, I take a long swig in the hope it'll calm me down. It's not very strong, but the sweetness should help. I know, I *know*, I'm overthinking again. It may not come to that.

Jacques is adamant he'll only be in Paris for a short time, a maximum of a week he says, but I don't buy it. Once he goes back, will he want to return to Australia? Will our relationship be over? I heave a sigh and rest my head against the chair.

"I heard that." Penny plops down on the other chair with a glass of red. "Stop thinking, Jane."

The kitten jumps but returns to his curled-up position, his purring vibrating against my legs. Gosh, I love this little ball of fur. He's become an instant part of our family, making it near complete. I say 'near' because, well...one day I'd love a little mini-Jacques. Or a mini-me.

"I can practically hear the cogs turning," Penny continues. In my periphery I see her glance at me with narrowed eyes. "I swear I can see smoke coming out of your ears too." She grins and sits back, sipping her wine.

"Ha ha." I reach across and push her arm. "You're right though, I *was* thinking. I hate my brain sometimes."

"Let me guess," Penny places her glass on the table, "you're thinking once Jacques goes to Pairs he won't come back to you."

I glance at her, deadpan. "How the hell do you know so much about me after such a short time?"

"Short time?" She scoffs and shifts on the chair, tucking her legs underneath her bottom. "It's been, what, eighteen months?"

I shrug. "I suppose so, but we don't chat that often. Anyway, that's not the point. I'm just annoyed that you're so in my head."

"And a good thing too. You are your worst enemy, Jane. Do you think Jacques would go to all the trouble to set you guys up here only to give it all up again?"

I sigh again and shake my head. "No, you're right. Once he commits to something, he sticks to it."

"Exactly, so stop thinking. You do realise he doesn't want to go back? His life is here, with you and Moe." She reaches across and scratches Moe under the chin. "Rather than overthinking about all the things it *isn't*, focus on what it *is*. His Papa is dying, and Jacques needs you. Don't forget that."

Jacques updated me on Marcel's condition and I know it's hit him hard, even if he hasn't admitted it. I'm not pushing him, he has to deal with it his way.

A scream from Henri sounds from inside followed by, "*Momie!*" from Amélie.

Penny groans and she huffs out a long sigh. "I can't even sit for five minutes." She sends me a tired smile before getting to her feet. "I'll be back soon, but tell your brain to shut up, okay? And *talk to Jacques*, tell him how you're feeling."

She picks up her wine glass and rushes off as Henri's screams reach ear-piercing levels. I wince and Moe wakes too, sitting on my lap and meowing up at me as though telling me to stop the crying. I wish I could Moe, I really wish I could. I pick him up and cradle him in the crook of my arm and stretch my legs out.

The sun has set, the streetlights have all blinked to life, and I can see a few bright stars twinkling in the inky sky, despite the light pollution. Henri stops crying and at the same moment the breeze stops. For a few seconds, it's blissfully silent apart from Moe's purring and the gentle lapping of waves in the distance.

The breeze is the first to start followed by some birds chirping in trees below, settling down for the night, followed by the faint sound of traffic.

I'm rightfully chided by Penny. I've been doing so much better at not overthinking Jacques' and my relationship, but my brain has gone into overdrive since learning he has to go back to Paris. He's booked a flight to return when Penny and Claude leave on Saturday. I still can't shake the feeling that he's going to be gone for more than a week.

I guess it shouldn't matter so long as he comes back.

But will he?

There's that intrusive thought again. Damn it to hell and back.

It's not Jacques I don't trust. It's his family. They're conniving and manipulative. They might've cut him from the family will, but that means nothing. I can't explain it. Something is off.

But Penny's right and I need to stop letting these thoughts overwhelm me. I *will* talk to Jacques because we promised to always communicate.

"*Bonsoir beauté.*" Jacques comes up behind me and kisses the top of my head.

I grin up at him. "Hey."

Moe wiggles out of my arm and jumps down, dashing back inside.

"Walk with me?" Jacques comes around and holds out his hand.

I take it and he pulls me up, leading me out of the apartment and to the elevators. "Where are we going?"

"It is a nice night for a walk along the beach. Claude said dinner will be a little while."

"Sounds perfect."

A few minutes later we arrive at the beach. Slipping off my sandals, I hold them in my free hand and step onto the coarse sand. The grains massage the soles of my feet. When Jacques does the same, I smile. To think that once upon a time he wouldn't take his shoes off for a picnic. He *has* come a long way.

As though reading my thoughts, he glances over and we share a reminiscent smile.

Hand in hand we wander the beach, not talking at first, just enjoying being together. The breeze catches in my hair and caresses my skin. *This* is the life. Walks on the beach whenever we want. No more bone-chilling winters or snow. I mean, snow is beautiful, but it's so freaking cold. And life is so much more laid back.

Looking across at Jacques, he has a small smile on his lips as the wind catches on his hair and blows it around. He fits in so well, it's like he was made for this life.

Penny's words run through my mind, and I take her advice. "Jack, are you okay?"

He glances at me, one eyebrow cocked. "Yes, why do you ask?"

"With everything going on with your family. Having to go back to Paris." I shrug for effect.

He nods and hums while he thinks. We continue walking for a few silent moments. Jacques tugs on my hand and leads me to the edge of the water where we stop, the lukewarm waves wrapping around our ankles. He turns to me, his gaze holding mine.

"You are worried?" He takes my hands.

My eyes threaten to fill with tears, but I blink them away. "A little." I draw in a breath of air, faint saltiness lingering on my tongue. "I'm scared you won't want to come home."

Saying the words out loud feels so stupid. We've been going strong for twelve months, but the moment his family appears I fall apart. I need help because this is getting silly.

"*Belle fille*," he whispers, tugging me closer so our bodies are touching, "you are the only one I want to come back to."

He leans in and kisses me with such promise, there's no way I can ever doubt this man.

"I have something for you." He steps back, digging into his pocket.

I draw in a deep breath to calm my racing heart. It's funny how a couple of words can make everything better. I do trust Jacques. Sometimes my head gets the better of me, that's all.

When Jacques reveals a small, round ring box my breath catches. Oh. My. Gosh.

Here?

Now?

"Jack—"

His smile is apologetic as he shakes his head. "This is not *the* ring, that will come later once everything with my family is sorted. But," he opens the lid to reveal a gold ring with an infinity symbol and a diamond-encrusted heart in the middle, "I heard promise rings were a thing."

He removes the ring and holds it out, the diamonds glimmering in the moonlight. "This is my promise to you that I will always come back for you, Jane Collins. Will you accept it until the time I can fulfil the promise and propose to you properly?"

"Oh Jack," there's no holding back my tears this time, "of course I accept."

He slides the ring on my finger, and we embrace. I breathe him in, the faint scent of pine and salt filling my senses.

This promise only instils in me the determination to make our relationship work, no matter what.

Chapter 9

Jacques

Claude and I shake hands with Hayden, our last interviewee for the Regional Manager position. It is three-thirty Thursday afternoon, our last interview of the day, *and* the last day of interviews. It has been a busy two weeks since Penny and Claude arrived. Longlisting candidates and then conducting interviews most days.

All positions have been filled, apart from the Regional Manager.

"Thanks for your time, mate." Hayden picks up his leather satchel, placing the strap over his shoulder.

"You will hear from us later this afternoon," I say.

Hayden's smile is confident as he lifts his hand in a wave and then strides to the elevator.

Once he is gone, I join Claude at the window. It is a clear day, with only a few wispy clouds in the sky.

It is still surprising that this is happening. The business I dreamt of opening for so many years is growing. I never thought I would ever be able to start one, let alone go international. The DuPont name has had such an adverse impact on my life, for so long I was certain I would be forever influenced negatively by it.

Now this. A positive outcome, in a country where no one knows me or my family.

I started on my own, now I have my best friend by my side. Together we have so many plans to make Solutions Exécutives great. This is even more motivation to keep my trip short. One week. That is all.

I turn back and take in the office with a smile. Almost everything is set up. All we need now is stationary supplies and computers. If I order everything before I leave for Paris, they will arrive next week while I am away. It means we must hire a Regional Manager today so they can be around to receive the shipment and sort it.

"What did you think of Hayden?" I ask, breaking out of my thoughts.

"I like him." Claude leans on the window with his shoulder. "Add him to the shortlist. Are you worried about why he left his job?"

I go over to the table and add Hayden's name to the list as I mull over Claude's comment. Hayden ticked all the boxes. He is still young, probably late twenties, enthusiastic, and has excellent experience. He has worked under his CEO father in a real estate business since he left high school.

"No, I am not worried." I sit on the edge of the desk facing Claude. "If he has been with the family business for so long, it is possible he is ready to go out on his own. I know what that is like." Claude nods in understanding. "But if you are worried, his reference checks should clear things up."

Claude takes his phone out of his pocket. "Yes, true. I'll make the calls now."

While Claude does that, I go over the shortlist again, but I keep going back to Hayden. He has the most relevant skills, but I cannot help wondering if Claude's concerns are valid. Are my instincts off? The last time I did not listen to him, Francine made my life extremely stressful.

"References check out," Claude says a few moments later, putting his phone away. "He even put his own father down, no bad blood there."

I sigh in relief. "What was his reason for leaving then?"

"Change of scene and society or something." Claude grins. "You were right."

"You had reason to doubt. So," I hold up the list, "who do you think is the best fit?"

We settle at the desk again and spend the next half an hour discussing each candidate, finally agreeing on Hayden. The added advantage is that he can start straight away. Saturday I will be flying out to Paris, and the opening of this branch is set for the following week. I can rest easy knowing someone will be here to finalise everything in time for the staff starting on opening day.

What is that phrase I heard Claude use the other day? Out of the frying pan and into the fire? An odd expression, but unfortunately relevant for Hayden. I will not be here to welcome him and help him settle into the role. He must dive in headfirst, and all our contact will be done online. It will be a test to see how he works without someone watching over him. I am not a micromanager and would prefer he hit the ground running.

Another expression I have adopted, this time from Jane.

"I think we'd be stupid not to hire Hayden," Claude says. "He seemed like an easy-going guy. He'll fit right in. Who's going to call him? We should call the unsuccessful ones too."

"Leave it with me," I grab the list from him, "I will do it. Did you not say you and Penny had plans?"

Claude nods and gets to his feet. "Thanks, and yes, we do. Don't forget you and Jane are babysitting."

"I have not forgotten." I swallow, feeling unprepared. I have never had to look after children before.

Despite the fact Jane and I both want children, what if I am not cut out for it? I could be a terrible father.

"Great, thanks." Claude goes over to the elevator and presses the button. He turns back and asks, "Are we still off to Moreton Island tomorrow?"

"Yes." I take out my phone. "We must leave early so I would recommend not staying out too late."

Tomorrow is our final opportunity to be together as friends. It is also nearing the end of Jane's and my month-long vacation. She will start her new job on Monday, so by the time I return from Paris we will be back to the busy routine of only seeing each other in the mornings and evenings.

The elevator door opens. "*Oui*, Papa." Claude chuckles as he steps inside.

Shaking my head, I wave him off then get to work making phone calls. I call Hayden first.

"Thanks mate," Hayden says when I tell him he has the job, "you won't regret it."

"I hope not. I mentioned in the interview that I am needed in Paris for one week and must leave Saturday. You will be required to keep on top of things here, and I will make sure I provide you with the details you need. My flight is in the evening. Will you be available for a quick meet-up in the afternoon so I can leave the keys with you?"

"Sure thing, I'm around all day."

"Okay, I will message you tomorrow with a time. I apologise for having to leave you on your own, I do not usually work like this."

Hayden chuckles. "Don't sweat it, Jacques. You're leaving the company in capable hands. As long as I know what needs to be done, it'll get done."

"Thank you. I will organise a Zoom call on Monday to go over everything."

"Sweet, thanks again. I'll wait to hear from you."

We hang up then I call the unsuccessful applicants. When that is done, I make a list of everything I will need to give Hayden before I leave. Keys, company credit card, email and database access, and a laptop.

Still a lot to do and so little time.

◆◆◆◆◆◆◆◆◆◆

Jane plops down on the sofa next to me. I rest my arm across her shoulders as she snuggles into my side. Moe is lying on his back, tucked in between my left side and the armrest of the sofa, all four legs splayed.

It has been an educational evening looking after Amélie and Henri. I did not expect our first official evening as babysitters to be so trying. Amélie did not want to go to sleep, and Henri would not stop crying.

Is this an omen? Proof that maybe I *will* be a bad father? One night with two kids and now I doubt everything.

Panic makes my chest tighten because tonight it occurred to me just how big a job it is to raise children. A child can do so little for themselves, they are so reliant on their parents. If I screw up, *they* could become screwed up. My family is proof of that, and I do not want to inflict that on my future child.

"They're asleep," Jane says with a sigh. "How do Penny and Claude do this *every* day?"

"I have no idea." Since we always agreed to be honest, I add, "Does it make you question...things?"

I suddenly feel inept. In the last year, I have been getting better at speaking my thoughts, but Jane feels strongly about children. I am worried about what I say because what if I upset her?

"What things?" She yawns.

"Children."

She stops mid-yawn, her mouth snapping shut. "Well, no. You?" Her eyes widen, but she does not appear annoyed or upset.

I contemplate my next words carefully. "It scares me," I say, feeling vulnerable.

Jane sits upright, alert now. "Okay." She bites her lip. "Any reason why?"

I tell her my concerns, and then in a rush, I add, "This does not mean I am changing my mind." I shuffle around to face her, disturbing Moe in the process. "It just means I do not want to rush into it."

To my relief, she laughs. "Hey," she crawls over to me, her eyes dancing with amusement, "I thought *I* was the overthinker here?"

"I cannot let you have all the fun."

"I appreciate you telling me." She sits back. "But we have no reason to rush this, right? When we're ready, we'll talk it through and make a plan. We're in this together."

I breathe a little easier, the panic starting to ease. "As always, you are right."

"I know." She shuffles off the sofa and gets to her feet.

I stand also and reach for her hand, turning her to me. I lean in to kiss her, pouring everything I have into it. Reminding her she is all I want and need.

"I love you, Jack," she whispers when we pull away. "Make sure you come back from Paris in one piece, okay? Don't let your family bully you."

"I will not let them." I tuck her soft, blonde hair behind her ears. "My family is here now."

Chapter 10

Jane

My skin tingles as Jacques runs his hands over my back, arms, and neck, massaging sunscreen into my skin. His touch leaves a burning sensation in its wake and it's *not* because of the hot sun.

When his warm lips press against the spot between my neck and shoulder, a shiver traipses down my spine. I turn my head to capture his lips and he settles down beside me without breaking the kiss. He gathers me into his arms, and we fall back onto the sandy towel. He holds me tight, his skin warm against mine, as I devour the heavenly taste of salt and sunshine on his lips.

With Claude and Penny walking the white sand with the kids, we have this blissful time together. Making up for lost time. It's hard to believe the month we had off is coming to an end. I don't resent Jacques for being busy, especially considering so much of *why* he's been busy was to surprise me.

I only wish we could have done more. Late-night walks on the beach. A trip to Tamborine Mountain. Perhaps a weekend trip to Cairns. Maybe next holiday.

After a long, blissful few moments of making out, I pull away and stare into Jacques' eyes, committing to memory the shining glow of love and tenderness in them. The warm breeze catches on my hair and caresses my skin, the sound of the waves lapping at the shore soothing.

"Thank you for today." I reach up to swipe a lock of dark hair from his forehead. "It's been amazing."

Jacques mentioned we were going to Moreton Island but didn't say what he'd planned. Of course, he thought of everything. Booked the ferry, packed lots of food and drinks, even organised kayaking and snorkelling activities. We went kayaking when we first arrived, and we'll be snorkelling after lunch.

"I am sorry we did not enjoy many more days like this," Jacques says.

"It's okay. You've done so much by sorting out our lives here. I appreciate everything you've given up."

He smiles in relief and gathers me in his arms once more, making short work of kissing me senseless yet again. I will never tire of this man.

It's only when we hear an *ahem* that we pull apart. Penny is shaking her head and grinning while Claude's cheeks burn bright red.

"Did you enjoy your walk?" I sit up and rest my arms on my knees.

Jacques chuckles beside me and lays back on his towel, hands behind his head. Claude joins him and they start talking.

"It was great." Penny places the pram and stroller facing me with the sun behind them. Amélie is asleep in the stroller, a thumb in her mouth. She's adorable in a frilly pink and white bathing suit and a pink hat. Henri is in the pram, covered by a light sheet.

Penny sits next to me and leans back on her elbows, staring out over the ocean. "This place is magical."

I hum in response and follow her example, taking in the stunning view of the white sand and the Tangalooma wrecks in the aqua-blue water. Crowds of people wander to and from the ferry. A lot of them go off to do their own thing but most suit up to snorkel among the wrecks. The centre of the island is populated and built up, even offering four-wheel driving for those who desire it.

After a few moments of silence, I glance across at Penny. "I'm going to miss you guys when you go back to Paris."

Penny sits up. "We'll miss you too, Jane. Especially now that your life is here for good." She sighs, a frown tugging on her lips.

"We'll still visit often. Would you think about moving back here?"

"No," Penny shakes her head, "Claude and I both love Paris too much. Australia doesn't feel like home anymore. Yeah, my family is here, but we're not super close. Visiting once a year is enough. I get a little wistful when I come to places like this and the Gold Coast. Sometimes I have a fleeting moment where I wonder if Claude and I could make it work. Then I think of everything we have back home, and I know it wouldn't. We'd both be unhappy."

She looks at me hard before adding. "What about you guys? You're setting up life here, but things change. Paris will always—"

"Not going to happen." I shake my head. "I don't want to go back. Ever."

"What about Jacques?" Penny's voice has an edge to it.

Realising what I said, my cheeks turn warm. "Sorry, I didn't mean for that to sound so selfish, but I can't deny the truth. Jack is happy here, so," I shrug, "here is where we're staying."

Penny nods but she's worrying her lip with her teeth. She opens her mouth to speak but snaps it shut again.

"C'mon, spit it out," I say. "What's on your mind?"

Penny draws a pattern in the sand with her index finger. "Truthfully, I just want you to be prepared for anything. What if Jacques decides he can't settle here?"

Irritation skirts along my skin and I draw in a breath before responding so I don't say anything snarky. "The same could be said of me. If we lived in Paris—"

"You'd adapt," Penny interrupts. "It's who you are, Jane. You and me, we adapt to changing situations easier than Jacques, and even Claude." Penny rests a hand on my arm and smiles kindly. "I'm confident he'll be fine, he wouldn't have opened a new branch here if he didn't think he would be, but I only want you to be prepared for anything. He's different to you and me. He's not made of the strong Aussie stuff like we are."

I shake my shoulders and breathe out a shaky laugh. "Yes, true. He's a weak Frenchman, I get it now." I roll my eyes so it's clear I'm joking.

"Who are you calling weak?" Jacques says next to me, slipping his arm across my shoulders and planting a warm kiss on my cheek.

Penny chuckles and at the same moment, Amélie jerks awake in her stroller, rubbing her eyes with her little fists. She looks at me then Penny, giving us a toothy smile. She asks for water and Penny rises to grab it for her. Henri wakes soon after and starts wailing, marking an end to our conversation.

I take Jacques' hand, "Wanna go for a swim?"

He nods and we both get to our feet, running over to the water and diving into its warmth. Penny's words linger in my mind, but I don't let them bother me. She means well and she's right. Jacques isn't naturally built for life here, but I think she's underestimating him. He *will* adapt, and I daresay he already has.

❧❧❧ ❦❦❦

It's Saturday evening and we're at the departure gate. Everything is checked in and the boarding call should sound any minute.

It's been a full on day.

Penny did some last-minute shopping and packing, while Jacques and Claude met up with Hayden, the new Regional Manager. I haven't met him, but Claude and Jacques have been raving about him.

While Jacques chats to Claude and Penny, appearing to not have a single care, I'm sitting and willing my brain to stop thinking. Stop worrying. I've put on a brave face and a happy smile, but it's difficult.

I gaze at the ring on my finger, hoping the reminder of Jacques' promise will calm me down, but it doesn't. The fears he silenced are back with force.

Breathing in, I hold it for a few seconds, but it comes out in a whoosh when the boarding announcement sounds over the loud-speaker.

No, not now. My bottom lip wobbles and I bite it, trying to keep my emotions in check.

We all stand, and I force a smile. Claude is the first to come up and give me a long hug. He's like a brother to me and I'm going to miss him.

Penny is next, wearing a worried smile. She's been busy today, so we haven't spoken much.

"Did I overstep the line yesterday?" Penny's brow creases in worry.

"You always overstep the line," I joke. "But that's what I love about you because you mean well. I can be selfish sometimes and as much as I love this place, it's not only about me."

She smiles and comes in for a hug. "I'm going to miss you. Don't be a stranger."

We embrace for a long moment, and I sniff back threatening tears. Penny is always the one to put things into perspective, delivering harsh truths when I need them.

She pulls away, kisses my cheek, and then joins Claude in the growing queue. He has Henri in a holster on his chest, and Amélie is in her stroller.

Jacques is the last one to come up to me and he takes my face in both of his hands. No words are needed as he leans in and kisses me slowly, softly, passionately. Pouring all the unspoken words into it. The din of the airport—overhead announcements, passengers coming and going, long lines of people waiting to board—all fade into the background.

"I will see you Sunday next week," he says when he pulls away. He leaves a lingering kiss on my forehead and then whispers, "*Je t'ami*, Jane."

A little thrill starts at the base of my spine and spreads through my body. "I love you too, Jack. I'll see you next week."

He leans in to kiss me one last time before joining Claude, Penny, and the kids.

I wave and walk away. Standing around watching them inch towards the gate is my idea of torture. It's already hard enough saying goodbye, why prolong it? Much to my relief, as I make my way to the car the fears that were overwhelming me a few minutes ago stay at the airport.

On the drive home, I realise this is the first time in twelve months that Jacques and I have been apart. I suppose that's not helping my mental state. I'm going to miss him like crazy, and it's going to be weird being on my own again. But...I get a *whole week* to myself. The whole bed. *The whole apartment.*

It's not all doom and gloom. I'm going to stop worrying and enjoy a little bit of freedom.

Chapter 11

Jane

Newsflash. I still don't cook.

What can I say? Jacques loves cooking and he's a natural at it, why would I deprive him? But with him gone, I must fend for myself. It's not that I *can't* cook. When I lived alone I had to, but my skills are basic and I'm far from professional.

Last night, my first night alone, I ended up nibbling on cheese and crackers with a glass of red. I was too busy pining after Jacques to be hungry. I'm not pining so much now, having the *whole* bed to myself last night was bliss, but I do miss him. It does mean I have my appetite back and I ordered pizza tonight.

Sitting on the balcony staring out over the twinkling city lights and the dark ocean, I reach for a slice of pizza from the box on the small table next to me. Sheet lightning flashes across the clouds on the horizon as they roll in, a thunderstorm threatening.

As I nibble on the pizza slice, my phone beeps, and my heart skips. Jacques?

I pick it up to see it's from Regina telling me she's looking forward to me starting my new job tomorrow.

"Of course it's not Jack," I mutter under my breath.

He sent messages during his two stopovers, but he's on his final leg to Paris now. I won't hear from him until he's at his apartment, which will be early morning my time.

Typing a reply to Regina, I draw in a breath and release it, calming the nerves causing my stomach to twist and turn. It's daunting starting a new job, but I've got mixed feelings about tomorrow. It'll be great working with Regina again, but after learning Jacques had considered offering me a job, I wish I hadn't been so rash in accepting Regina's offer. I love the idea of Jacques and I working together.

Putting my phone aside, I pull my feet up onto the chair, grab a final slice of pizza and watch the storm roll in while I nibble it. The hairs on my arms stand on end as thunder rumbles across the sky and fork lightning strikes the ground a few metres away.

Seconds later rain pelts down, wind blows, and lightning gives an awesome display. In typical Queensland style, it passes quickly but there's a refreshing chill in the air. I'm a little calmer and more relaxed, so I hope this means I'll sleep well.

I need all my wits about me for my first day tomorrow.

I wake up with a start when my phone rings. Jacques!

Grinning, I reach across for my phone and my heart flips when I see his name on the screen. The time reads six a.m. which would be about right by the time he landed, got through international arrivals, and made it home.

I swipe the screen to answer. "Jack?"

"*Bonjour beauté.*"

He sounds tired but it only makes his voice deeper and huskier. A shudder ripples down my spine and an ache grows in my chest. I miss him.

"It's so good to hear your voice. How was your flight?"

"Long, but fine. How was your first day of work?"

"It's Monday morning here, I haven't started yet."

"Oh," he tsks on the other end, "yes of course. I have the days muddled. I hope your first day goes well."

"Thanks. I miss you already, Jack." I sigh and lay back down, staring at the ceiling.

"And I you." I hear a shuffling on the other end. "It will not be long before I am on the flight back to you."

"Good, because I need your cooking again. I ordered pizza last night and ate it all." It was delicious pizza, but I shouldn't have eaten the whole thing. "My self-control is at an all-time low and I may relapse tonight. I might turn into a balloon if I'm not careful."

Jacques chuckles.

"Maybe I'll go out to a sushi restaurant tonight instead," I say then yawn. "You must be shattered, Jack."

"I am, but I am happy to talk to you again." He yawns this time.

My grin spreads across my face. "Are you prepared for seeing your family?"

He's silent for a moment. "As ready as I will ever be. Tomorrow I will go into the office and then meet up with Maman after work to discuss Papa's condition. I will probably visit him at the same time."

He goes silent again. At first, I assume he's thinking about his family, but he's silent too long and his breathing turns heavy.

"Jack?"

He stirs and draws in a sharp breath. "Yes?"

I chuckle. "Did you fall asleep?"

"Sorry, the jetlag is taking over."

I sit up and position myself on the edge of the bed. "It's okay, you should go to bed. I love you, Jack."

"I love you too, Jane."

As we hang up, electrical currents surge through me, making every single nerve ending tingle. I don't think I'll ever get sick of hearing him tell me he loves me in French *or* English.

Fully awake now, I take advantage of the extra time. I go for a swim first then come upstairs to change for work, have breakfast, and fill Moe's food and milk bowls. I leave for work at eight thirty a.m. and grab myself a coffee on the way, arriving at my new office at quarter to nine.

Regina is waiting by the office door when I arrive. She's dressed in oversized clothes again, but I'll never forget the figure she hides. This woman is *not* who I thought she was. Today she's wearing a colourful, flowery maxi dress, and sandals, with makeup that is, as usual, perfectly applied. Her red hair is piled high on her head, and she has dangly earrings in her ears, a bulky necklace, and multiple bracelets around her wrists.

I push on the door and step through, sending her a bright smile. "Morning Reg,"

"Jane." She beams and holds out a folder. "Welcome. Here's your induction pack. Follow me and I'll show you to your desk."

Only a few words, but already it's like she's had a total personality transplant from when we met for lunch. That new side of Regina will be forever etched in my brain. We haven't spoken much since. I assume she's been busy.

Seeing her now, looking and sounding like her old self, I breathe easier. Regina is in boss mode, the person I'm familiar with and like most. Perhaps we'll only ever be workplace friends.

She takes me past some office doors, a kitchen, and toilets, before entering an open office space. There are eight pods with walls between them, tall enough to look over but giving workers some privacy.

She stops in front of a desk, assumingly mine, that has a laptop still in its box and some stationary supplies.

"You're the first one here," Regina says, "so set yourself up and settled. We'll do a group induction once everyone else arrives."

I nod and Regina turns to leave but stops and turns back. "How's Jacques?"

"Oh, he's fine. He's just flown back to Paris—"

The words die on my tongue when Regina's eyebrows rise in question, curiosity on her face. Bugger.

"He has, has he?" She shuffles back and pulls out a chair from the desk next to me, sitting on it. "Why is that, hmm?"

The worries I've been fighting come to the surface again. How does Regina do it with one look and doubt in her tone?

"Don't start, please." I don't mean to sound like I'm begging but I don't need her making this worse. "He's only gone for a week. His father is sick."

Most normal people would show concern. Regina, I'm learning, is far from normal. Her interest only grows and a sly smile spreads across her face, reminding me of a Cheshire cat.

"Yes, of course he is." Regina rolls her eyes and gets to her feet, her bracelets jangling.

She grins at me, shakes her head, tuts and leaves. So much for old Regina. New Regina is already peeking through and I'm not sure I like her.

Rattled, I grit my teeth and turn back to my desk, opening the laptop box.

Don't overthink. Do not overthink.

Chapter 12

Jacques

It is strange waking up in my Paris apartment. My head is fuzzy with jetlag but otherwise, I slept well and I am ready for a day of work.

I followed Claude's advice and wrote the statement to start the process of damage control. Claude's journalist contact worked his magic and the negative articles are becoming fewer. While I am here, I will meet with the contact to talk about ways we can stay in a positive light.

My focus, while I am here, is to also have meetings with my staff members. Some one-on-one time to discuss their career goals, and some meetings to discuss the future of Solutions Exécutives.

While Claude's position is to always be the available executive while I am absent, I have learned that employees want their CEO to show an interest. Not just online, but in person. It is supposed to build trust. There is still so much to learn, but if I want to be a modern man with modern views, I must take action now. Make sure my team members are being listened to and feel like part of the company.

Getting out of bed, I open the curtains and smile at the city streets covered in snow. It has been a cold winter, just how I like it. As much as I enjoy my life in Australia, I will miss the cold and the snow.

As I prepare for work, there are reminders of Jane everywhere. Once upon a time I resented this apartment and the fact I had no choice when I bought it. Now I like it...it is homey. Paintings and pictures on the walls. The shelves around the TV have been bulked out with not just my books, but also hers. I now have rugs, throw cushions, and little knickknacks dotted around.

I arrive at the office at eight a.m., before anyone else, coffee in hand. When I am seated at my desk, the first thing I do is schedule a whole team meeting for later this afternoon. Next, I send individual meeting invites to the staff.

One hour later, I find myself staring at the hundreds of unread emails in my inbox. My eyes flick to a pile of files on the corner of my desk, close to toppling point, and I sigh. My goal was to run a paperless office, yet somehow the files keep coming.

Since this is the head office, I must set an example for all future offices to follow. To prove that I do not run my business like Entreprises DuPont, I want to do all I can to protect the environment. Going paperless was supposed to be the first, and easiest, goal we achieved. We were going well at one point, but something has gone awry.

Reaching for my coffee, I sip it while flicking through the top three files. I soon realise this is a job Hugo, the assistant Claude and I share, can do. Most of it is data entry, with a handful of phone calls, and then the files can be archived. After sending Hugo an instant message with the job request, I send an all-staff reminder about going paperless, making sure to include Hayden. He can share to the Australian staff once they start.

A few minutes later Hugo comes in to grab the files and leaves again. The door closes and my desk phone rings.

I slip into French easily when I answer, relieved to be able to speak without having to rethink everything I say. I am more natural and professional.

"I'm looking for Jacques DuPont?" A female voice says. "I was told to call this number."

There is something familiar about the voice, but I cannot pinpoint it.

"This is he. How may I help?"

An instant message pops up on my screen from Hugo.

Your Maman left a message. She wants you at the hospital at 2 p.m.

The woman says something but I am distracted by Hugo's message and do not hear her. Quietly muttering under my breath, annoyed at Maman's entitlement, I send a reply to Hugo.

Please return her call and tell her I will be there at 5 p.m. as planned.

Maman still expects me to drop everything for her, but I will not. I already told her the times I am available.

"Are you there Jacques?"

I blink a couple of times and minimise Hugo's message. "Sorry, what were you saying?"

"Oh, I was just saying how wonderful it is to hear your voice. My God, it's been so long since—"

I shake my head, confused. "Excuse me, but who is this?"

She laughs nervously. "I'm sorry, I got ahead of myself. When my husband, Tavish, told me he wanted to hire someone to help our business, I thought of you after the recent news article. I could barely contain my excitement."

Who is this person? Am I missing something?

"I am sorry, madame, have I met you or your husband before?"

There is a soft huff on the other end followed by another laugh. "I'm so sorry. Tavish would like to set up a meeting to discuss our business and how to improve."

And now she is avoiding my question altogether? I am confused, but keeping to the topic, I reach for my mouse and open the email calendar. "Of course, do you have a preferred day or time?"

I have time this afternoon before the staff meeting, so I slot them in. When we hang up, I am more confused than ever.

Shaking my head, I push the thoughts aside and focus on the never-ending list of tasks I need to address. The morning consists of one more meeting, making a start on sorting through my unread emails, and taking calls. Our client base is growing day by day with new ones, including others coming over from Entreprises DuPont. It will be interesting seeing my family again and whether they will reveal anything about the company's downward trajectory.

It is a rush to eat lunch before my next appointment, the one scheduled over the phone this morning.

A knock sounds at my door at two p.m. It opens, and Hugo comes in to announce the clients. I stand as a tall, broad gentleman with a bushy red beard enters. His hair is also red but tinged with grey. He has a wide smile and rosy cheeks.

He strides up to my desk and holds out a hand. "You must be Jacques," he says in a strong Scottish accent. "I'm Tavish Kilpatrick."

I take his hand and we shake. "Nice to meet you, Tavish." Slipping into English is much easier nowadays. I let go of his hand and gesture to one of the seats on the opposite side of my desk. "Please take a seat."

A woman enters, shutting the door after her and smiles at me shyly. I am lowering myself into my chair but one look at her and I fall into it with a gasp. It cannot be!

"Thank you for taking the time to see me today, Jacques," Tavish says, but I barely hear him, "this is my wife Aimée."

It has been many years, over twenty, so she would have to be in her mid-forties now, but there is no mistaking that face. Those soft, caring light brown eyes. That shy smile.

The au pair from my childhood.

She looked after me for four years and left when I was eleven. She was the first person I connected to. Despite how young I was when she left, I never forgot her or the kindness she showed. She managed to plant something deep inside me that stopped me from turning into a worse version of myself.

The phone call earlier. It was her? That was why she had acted so strange and why her voice was familiar. Her French accent might have weakened over the years and she now has a Scottish lilt, but there is no way I can forget it.

What is going on? Why is she here? Was she not sick?

I cannot form words. The shock of seeing her has shaken me to the core. I have so many questions, but now is not the time to ask.

She offers me an apologetic smile and holds out a hand. "It's lovely to see you again, Jacques."

"Again?" Tavish glances from me to Aimée.

"Yes," Aimée sits next to her husband and beams at me, "I was his au pair when he was a boy. Remember I told you?" Her eyes shine with tears and a stray one slides down her cheek. She wipes it away and then averts her gaze.

Tavish's eyes light up and he grins. "You don't say, what a small world we live in."

"Very small." There is a bitterness in my tone, but despite that, a pocket of warmth settles in my chest at the knowledge that she talked about me after she left.

Tavish does not notice my bitterness, but Aimée does. Her head snaps up and her gaze meets mine, an apology in her eyes that tells me she has a lot to say.

A lot I want to know.

Why did she leave without saying goodbye? Was she not as sick as I thought?

In front of Aimée, I am a vulnerable little boy again. I am transported back to being eleven years old. It was not long after my Grand-mère passed away. I knew Aimée was sick but did not know what was wrong. One day she left without saying goodbye.

Tavish grins. "Well, well, well, that is braw!"

I furrow my brow. "Braw?" It is not a word I recognise.

"It's Scottish slang for 'amazing'," Aimée explains, looking at her husband with a loving smile. "It took me a long while to learn their unusual words."

Tavish chuckles and takes Aimée's hand. "Now, shall we get to business?"

"Yes." I adjust my tie and sit straighter in my seat, a futile attempt to grapple for some semblance of normalcy and fight this vulnerability tightening my chest. "How can I help you today?"

Turns out Tavish and Aimée took over a small, struggling office supplies business from Aimée's sister and brother-in-law, but it is not doing so well. To make it a success again, they need our help.

As we talk, I type notes on my computer. At the end, I draw up a contract that covers everything involved, including the costs. My business motto is still around affordability and transparency. I require a small deposit to begin the work, and my company receives a percentage of the business income for a set amount of time, as agreed upon before anything is signed.

Worst case scenario, if a business fails and is forced to sell, or the owners decide to sell, I get a percentage of the sale. I try very hard not to go down this route unless all other avenues have been exhausted. I have never had to do this yet. Of course, there was the sale of Claude's business before I went to Australia. In this case though it was his choice, not because we had exhausted all avenues.

When the contract is digitally signed and everyone has been sent a copy, we all stand and I shake hands with Tavish.

"Thank you, Jacques." Tavish lets go of my hand and steps out from the chair. "I look forward to working with you." He touches Aimée's arm. "Are you ready?"

"I'd like to speak to Jacques for a moment." She places her hand over his. "Shall I meet you downstairs?"

Tavish nods then with a final wave and a smile, turns and leaves. Aimée stays put, staring at me. My mouth is dry, and my mind is blank.

Aimée is holding her handbag in both hands as she shuffles from foot to foot. "It's so good to see you. You've grown into such a handsome and successful man."

Overwhelmed, I pinch the bridge of my nose and breathe in deeply. "Why—?" but the words die on my tongue, vulnerability taking over, rendering me speechless.

Why did you leave me, is what I want to say, but I feel so weak, so...childish.

Aimée lowers her face and draws in a breath. "The article about your company and you and your success, it was the first time I had seen you since..." She clears her throat, but the words do not need to be spoken.

"Since you left without saying goodbye?" I did not intend to say this aloud, but the words are out before I can stop them. I mutter a curse, then add, "I apologise, that was out of line."

Aimée comes up to me and rests a soft, comforting hand on my arm. "Please don't apologise."

I release a slow breath. "Why are you only coming forward now?"

"I have not been in the country. I have been in Scotland for over twenty years now and we only returned to Paris late last year to take over the business. Jacques," she steps back, "we have much to talk about, and I'm sure you have many questions. Would you like to have lunch one day?"

"I would like that." I go back to my desk and check my calendar. We schedule lunch for Wednesday, then she leaves.

After the staff meeting, the rest of the afternoon is a blur of activity. I do not have time to comprehend what has happened. Before I know it, I am at the hospital and striding down the hallways towards Papa's ward. The sterile smell irritates my nostrils.

Even though I have had plenty of time to prepare for this visit, I have forgotten everything.

When I reach the ward, Maman is waiting for me outside the nurse's station. She appears tired. Older, even. Not her sophisticated self.

I will never forget the day I saw them, in Papa's office after Jane left. The contempt. The betrayal. We all made our decisions that day and I have no regrets about mine.

"Jacques," Maman says, her eyes shining with unshed tears, "it is lovely to see you again." A normal mother would open her arms for an embrace. My Maman steps up and places a kiss on my cheek.

When she steps back, her pose perfect as ever, she folds her hands in front of her. Up close, I see bags under her eyes. Her hair is neat but not styled. Her clothes are pressed and unwrinkled, not the stylish ones she would normally wear.

"Where are Céleste and Rémy?"

"They will visit later. We will meet as a family another day. Your Papa wanted to see you alone. He is expecting you." She gestures to the closed door of his private room.

He is expecting you. So professional despite being in a hospital. Some things never change.

I turn to the door, draw in a deep breath, then push down on the handle and step into his room. Closing the door behind me, I glance around to find Papa sitting in bed propped up by pillows, head lolled to the side as he snores quietly.

He is a skeleton, nothing but skin and bone. Sunken eyes, jaundiced skin, yet still wearing stylish pyjamas. He is not the powerful man I remember. I step forward, my shoes squeaking on the floor. Papa jerks awake and turns his head to me, unblinking. He holds out his hand, a weak smile tugging at his lips.

I do not remember the last time he smiled.

I sit beside the bed but ignore his hand.

"Jacques, my son," Papa says weakly in French, his voice raspy like he has not used it in a long time. "You are here."

"Why did you need me here so urgently?" I ask, sticking to French. Folding my hands in my lap, I keep my expression neutral.

My heart is racing and skipping inside my chest. First Aimée, and now Papa. Two unpleasant memories of my past. In a way.

Aimée is a pleasant memory, but her leaving wasn't.

Papa rests his hands on his lap. "I deserve your coldness. I have not been a good father. While I do not expect your forgiveness, I hope you will accept my apology."

I blink at him, unexpected tears pricking my eyes. I was not expecting an apology. I have heard the prospect of death can do this to people.

It does not fix anything, but the apology is not unwelcome.

"Thank you, Papa." My voice cracks and I clear my throat.

I have so many questions, but I am tongue-tied.

"There is much to say, Jacques, but before your brother and sister arrive, I must tell you something important. I did not want to tell anyone else until you know."

I stare at him, unable to think what it might be. I nod for him to continue.

"I never updated the will, Jacques." Papa's eyes are focused on me.

"Excuse me?"

Papa lowers his gaze and runs his hand over the blanket, smoothing out a crease. "You heard me. The will was never updated. When I am gone, Entreprises DuPont is yours and yours alone."

Chapter 13

Jacques

I stare at Papa for a long moment. His words sink in and I stand, the chair scraping back on the smooth, hard floor.

"I do not understand." I rake my hand through my hair, pacing back and forth.

"What is difficult about it? You are familiar with the family will, nothing has changed."

"Precisely." I stop pacing and glare at him. "You tried to stop me from succeeding in my own business. Led me to believe you cut me out of the will because I would not do what you wanted. You *disowned* me because I dared to do my own thing. Now this? What game are you playing? How can I believe anything you say?"

I ball my hands into fists, hitting them against my legs. I could have ignored the pleas to visit Papa before he passes, I owe them nothing, but I am not that sort of person. I believe in second chances, in letting people prove they have changed. I would have had regrets if I did not come back.

To my surprise, Papa appears contrite. "There is no game, Jacques. I was wrong. I did not handle the situation well. Seeing the success of your business has made me very proud." He smiles at me. "Facing death makes a man think and I do not want to leave this earth without knowing the family empire is in good hands."

My legs grow weak and I stumble back over the chair, falling into it with a sigh. I do not remember a time when Papa ever told me he was proud of me. All I remember is constant criticism, and not constructive.

"Your brother is a terrible businessman. I thought I could entrust the company to him while I was ill and if he did well, I would change the will, but..." he sighs and lifts his hands, palms up. "You have seen the news articles?" I nod. "All lies." He folds his hands on his lap. "The company is sinking under his leadership. I cannot rely on him to make Entreprises DuPont great again. *You* can if your success is anything to go by."

"At what cost? I refuse to let my business fail for a company I want no part of."

"Not even for the family?" Papa's eyes flash and his mouth curves down in a deep frown. He may be dying and showing signs of remorse, but he is and always will be the same cold-hearted brute.

"Not for *this* family." I sit straight in my chair, holding Papa's gaze, making sure my message is clear. "Ever since I was little, you and Maman have done nothing but control my life. I refuse to let that happen again. I have my own life and my own company, that is all I need."

Papa's nostrils flare and his face turns red. "This company has been around for over one hundred years and the oldest DuPont son has always done his duty by following in his father's footsteps. If Rémy was capable, I would have overlooked this, but he is not. It is your turn now, whether you like it or not. The will is final, I am not changing it again. My time is limited, I do not want to worry about legalities in my final days."

I grind my teeth, trying to keep control of the raging anger bubbling low in my belly. "I will sell the moment the company is in my name."

Papa's smile is sly. "Have you forgotten the clause that says the company cannot be sold while your Maman is alive?"

Mon Dieu, how could I have forgotten? This is not going how I planned at all. I was going to come in, pay my respects and leave. Why is nothing ever simple?

Papa tuts. "That girl you are seeing, the plain one, she has changed you. She is very much like—"

He stops and stares at the wall, a strange, maniacal smile appearing on his lips for a split second before disappearing again. He shakes his head, as though ridding a memory, then moves his gaze to me. "You are spineless, boy." His tone is cold. "That is why I refuse to change my mind about the will. It is time to man up and run a *real* company, a reputable one."

My spine stiffens and I clench my jaw. There are many things I want to say. Tell him how wrong he is. That Jane is everything he is not. That my company is ten times more reputable than his. I want to tell him about seeing Aimée today too.

I do not say any of it. I am done with pointless arguments, which this conversation is becoming, full of lies and excuses.

"How am I supposed to run my own company and yours from Australia?" I hope to give off the impression that his words do not affect me.

His cold gaze holds mine. He is set in his ways...determined. "That is not my problem. The will is not changing, it is what it is. I only wanted you to be aware before I...pass."

Restless, I stand again, both of my hands gripping my hair. "Does Maman know? What about Céleste and Rémy?"

Papa's lips press into a thin line and he averts his gaze.

"They do not," I say matter-of-factly. "Maman signed the changed will, did she not?"

Papa waves away my question as though the answer is obvious. "I did not sign when she did, I only witnessed her signature. I was going to get mine witnessed by the family lawyer, but I destroyed it after I changed my mind."

I shake my head and cover my face with my hands. I need time to think and figure out how to deal with this.

"I must go." I let my arms fall to my sides. "I will be leaving Paris late Friday, but I can come by if you need me for any other legalities."

I would rather avoid seeing my family again, but since there is no way out of this mess, I want to make it as seamless as possible.

"I would like to rest anyway." Papa presses a button to lay the bed flat. "I recommend you reread the will and make sure you understand it. I would like to see you tomorrow along with your Maman and siblings. I need you here when I tell them the news."

I nod once. "I will be here after work, the same time as today. Make sure they are not late." I turn and leave without a goodbye to him, or Maman who is still waiting outside.

There must be some way out of this, there *must*.

Rather than going straight home as planned, I detour to the DuPont building. I still have the security pass, and Papa keeps a copy of the will in the filing cabinet in his office. I must read it before tomorrow as I do not have the copy Papa originally gave me.

Two hours later it is dark, and snowflakes are falling outside the floor-to-ceiling windows when I close the leather folder and stretch my arms above my head. Rubbing my eyes, I stand and pace Papa's office. This change of plan alters everything I have laid out in Australia.

Stopping in front of a window overlooking the City, the lights twinkle through the falling snow. In the distance, the Arc de Triomphe glows golden. To the left, the Tour Eiffel starts sparkling as the time ticks over to eight p.m. I am reminded of Jane and the 'date' Claude and Penny had set us up on. So much has changed since that moment. The pain of missing her settles in the centre of my chest.

How do I handle this while keeping our plans?

Placing my forearm on the cool window, I rest my head on it and sigh. My warm breath fogs up the glass then clears.

It has been over one year since I read the will and I had forgotten a lot of the details. The house and all its contents will be left to Maman. The family business is left to me, but my siblings must have positions within it. Céleste does not work for the company, so this surprises me. What position would I give her?

The final clause has me baffled. While most of the family funds will be left to Maman, since me and my siblings have received our trust funds, a small portion will still be divided among 'all natural children of Marcel DuPont'. That was the precise wording. I would have thought names would be specified, but it is not like I can question it. Papa has made it clear he will not change the will, so what is the point?

My only worry now is how I am going to tell Jane. I think right now I need to keep it to myself until I know what I am going to do.

⟫⟫ ⟪⟪

T he next morning, I wake up at six a.m. and go for my morning jog. First light of day on the horizon colours the heavy clouds a light grey.

The snow crunching under my feet is the only sound, interrupted by the occasional car of other early risers going to work. My breath puffs out in visible clouds and my shoes leave footprints in the snow.

Buildings, cars, and fences are white. Windows are frosted over. The Tour Eiffel pops in and out of view as I navigate the streets following my usual loop, which takes me back to my apartment building.

When I reach it half an hour later, it starts snowing. The small snowflakes fall lightly from the sky, settling on cars, buildings, in my hair, and stinging my cheeks. Panting, I stop outside and look up and down the street, breathing in the fresh, chilly air.

Making my way upstairs, I get ready for work and then have breakfast and coffee before going into the office. I want to ring and talk to Jane, but she will still be at work. Instead, I text her and ask her to call me when she is free.

I arrive at the office before eight a.m. as I have a lot to do today, including many individual staff meetings. Jane messages me at nine a.m. and I FaceTime her, needing to see her.

Her smile lights up the screen when she answers, and everything is right in the world.

"*Bonjour beauté.*"

Jane's smile only grows. "Hey, how are you? Did everything go okay last night?"

"It was not so bad. How was your first day of work?"

Jane's smile disappears. "It was...interesting." Her brow creases. "Regina's different somehow."

"You told me after you had lunch with her that she seemed different."

"Yes," Jane taps her chin, "I thought it was just her 'social side'. But I don't think it is."

"You think it is not the job you hoped it would be?" I dismiss a reminder on my computer telling me I have a meeting with Hugo in ten minutes.

"I think it's too early to tell. I'll give it more time. It could also be because I'm not used to working with her. I have a lot to learn at this new job, new people to get to know. Did you know it takes a good six months to settle into a job? A whole *year* to feel like you belong."

Her eyes are wide and I cannot help but chuckle. "Is that so? I suppose you should give it at least one year then, yes?"

"I guess so." Her sigh drifts along the line and washes over me.

Hugo pokes his head into my office, but his eyes widen. "Sorry, I'm early, I will—"

I wave him in. "It is fine, Hugo, come in." I look back at the phone as Hugo settles in a chair opposite me, turning to glance out the window.

I don't miss the disappointment on Jane's face, but she still manages a bright smile. "It's okay, work beckons. We'll talk later?"

I nod, she blows me a kiss and we hang up.

⇝⇝ ⇜⇜

It is a busy but successful day. I had booked a lot of individual meetings today, and I got through about half of our small team. The rest are booked for tomorrow and Thursday.

When the day ends, I pack up and go to the hospital as organised. When I enter Papa's room, the entire family is already there. My gaze drifts to Rémy and Céleste, two people I barely recognise.

It is strange seeing them again, but stranger to call them brother and sister. While I remained at home, schooled by tutors, and taught the family business, my brother and sister had different lives.

Céleste has become a lot like Maman. Petite, regal, snobbish. Her hair is longer, coming to her shoulders, and her clothes are more modern. With only a two-year age gap between Céleste and me, she was Maman's *petite princesse*. Spoilt and given everything she could ever need or want. I do not remember having a relationship with her. She was sent to a prestigious private boarding school from a very young age for the best education. I only saw her during the holidays, but she quickly grew into a younger version of Maman and wanted nothing to do with me.

Rémy, unsurprisingly, is much like Papa and me. Tall, dark, broad, square-jawed. He was a surprise, an unwanted child. Born seven years after me, he too was sent away to boarding school. This one was less prestigious. Maman and Papa did not care about his education, they only wanted to send him away and forget about him. I only saw him once a year, sometimes less. He was born around the time Aimée came on the scene.

It is no wonder my siblings and I are strangers to each other now. Our parents did everything in their power to keep us apart. While I doubt I will ever be able to have a relationship with Céleste, as for Rémy...well, he is still young. Only twenty-seven and still so much to learn. Can I help him? Is it too late to be the big brother I never got to be?

"Ah, Jacques, there you are," Maman says in French.

I blink away my thoughts and turn my attention to her. She is more herself today. Her hair is freshly dyed and immaculately styled, wearing one of her stylish pantsuits with lots of jewellery.

"Let us get started," Papa says, but his voice holds no power. He has weakened since yesterday and his breathing is laboured. "We are here to discuss my last will and testament. I do not have long to live, and I want everything sorted."

Maman whimpers and goes over to him, clutching his hand. It takes enormous effort not to roll my eyes. The last time I saw them together, she appeared scared of his anger. I believed her to be afraid, but now she acts like this.

I do not know what I am expecting when Papa breaks the news about the will, but total disinterest is not it. A single shrug from Céleste. A sniff from Maman. A scoff from Rémy. That is all.

When Papa is resting, Maman by his side, Céleste leaves stating she has an important event to attend, and I take Rémy aside. I nudge his shoulder, inclining my head to the door, indicating we should talk. He nods and we go out into the hallway.

"So, *grand frère* back to save the day," Rémy sneers.

I sigh. This is not a good start. "No, Rémy, it is not like that."

He raises his eyebrows in question. "You still got everything, did you not? *Sanglant typique.*" He rolls his eyes. "You always were the favourite, is that not normal for the oldest child? You turned your back on this family for a so-called better life and that did not change Papa's mind either."

Favourite? Once upon a time, this would surprise me. Now, as I have recalled the childhood we had, I understand why it appears that way to him.

"I do not want everything," I say. "Do you think I want any of this? I did not go out on my own just to prove a point. I did so because I wanted to get away. For the record, Maman and Papa disowned me when I left the family company. Led me to believe the will had been changed and I was no longer in it. This is a surprise to me."

Rémy tsks. "Please, do not patronise me. They never let up about how you will make Entreprises DuPont great again, unlike me."

"Rémy, *I do not want the company,*" I emphasise the words, trying to get him to understand. "I told Papa this, asked him to give it to you, but he refused to change the will. He is punishing me for going out on my own, wants my company to fail. I would hand this company over to you if I could."

Rémy stares at me in confusion, like he is learning something new. He probably is. There is a vulnerability in his eyes. I never stopped to think about how his being sent away, made to feel so unloved and unwanted would affect him. Perhaps letting him run the company will help. He just needs to learn. I am happy to teach him if he is interested.

I must prove I am not like our father and genuinely want to help him.

Maybe we will connect over a drink.

One step at a time. For now, my focus must be on Entreprises DuPont and getting Rémy on board. If Papa does not have long left, I need to have a plan in place for when I am given ownership.

"Rémy." I step forward and level my gaze with his. "I do not want to run Entreprises DuPont, but the ownership will be given to me whether I like it or not. Just because I will own it means nothing, I still want *you* to continue running it."

Rémy steps back, shaking his head. "I told you not to patronise me. Why would I want to work under my brother who does not care about us?"

"I do care—"

He holds his hands up and starts walking backwards. "I do not want to hear your lies. Besides, the company is failing, why would I want to sail a sinking ship?"

"Because you care about it more than I do, and you want it to succeed. Under my guidance, I can help you to make that happen."

Rémy stops, eyeing me like he is considering it but laughs and shakes his head. "You nearly got me, *frère*. It will not happen. Have a good life."

One more shake of his head and Rémy leaves. He turns down a corridor but I rush after him.

"We are not done here, Rémy," I call after him a little too loudly. A couple of nurses scowl at me.

Rémy ignores me and keeps walking.

Chapter 14

Jane

"Moe, here kitty," I call out, shaking the bag of dry kitten food, "Moe, where are you?"

I catch the digital time on the microwave which reads eight fifteen a.m. Dang it, I haven't got time for a missing kitten. I couldn't find him last night though, his food is untouched, so I'm a little concerned. I'm certain he hasn't done his Houdini act again as I'm always super careful when I leave, but where can he be?

"Moe?" I call again but this time I'm interrupted by my phone ringing. I put the food down and retrieve my phone, grinning when I see Jacques' name on the screen. I answer with the camera on and a bright smile. "Hi!"

When the video loads, his drawn face comes into view. He has bags under his eyes and his hair is messy, as though he's run a hand through too many times. It's as though he's had the worst day in history.

"Holy hell you look like crap," I blurt.

This at least elicits a small laugh, which lightens his face. "It has been a difficult day, but seeing you again makes it better."

I grin. "Ditto. Do you want to talk about it? Seeing your family two days in a row is taking its toll, hey?"

His smile freezes but only for a second. "Something like that, but it was not so bad, I suppose."

"Oh, that's good. How about work? Everything running smoothly?"

That frozen smile returns but disappears quickly. "Everything is fine. Hayden messaged me a few minutes ago with photos of the office space. He is only waiting for the computers now. It is coming together well."

"Good, that's great."

The conversation is awkward, stilted and that's always a sign he's dealing with something. But I know Jacques, and he'll talk when he's ready, so I don't push.

"Hey, do you happen to know of any hiding spots where Moe might be?"

Jacques appears to relax as we change topics. "Is he missing?"

"Not missing per se, I'm certain he hasn't escaped. But he didn't eat last night, or this morning and I'm worried he's locked away or stuck inside somewhere."

"Have you checked the spare bedroom? I have found him under the bed in the far corner sometimes. It is very dark, so he is easy to miss."

"Oh, good idea!" I rush to the bedroom and kneel on the floor, turning on the phone torch. I shine it under the bed and sure enough, squeezed in the corner in his tiny loaf form, is Moe. Even from here, I can tell he's breathing too fast. "Found him." Panic builds up in my chest. "I think he's sick, Jack. Is there a vet near our apartment?"

"I am not sure, but if you think he is sick you must find one soon."

I'm aware of how much time I *don't* have but since Moe has been without food for over twelve hours, I'm reluctant to leave him for a whole day.

"I will, sorry to cut this short but I must go. I miss you, Jack. I can't wait to see you on Sunday."

There's a long pause on the other end. I sit back and look into the camera. Jacques is smiling but something is still off. Determined not to overthink or worry, I let it go.

"Me too." His smile is...sad?

A tiny voice in my head says, "He's only saying he's coming home but he won't," and I shut it up quick smart. I don't need these thoughts right now.

"Will we talk later?"

"Of course, I will call you during my lunch break."

We hang up and I go in search of the cat cage. We haven't had to use it yet but knew it would be a necessary purchase for the inevitable vet visit. I didn't expect it to be so soon though. Once I find it, I place it in front of the bed with the door open and food inside in the hopes Moe will be lured into it.

While I wait, I text Regina.

Kitten is sick, must find a vet ASAP. Will be a little late.

It's only day three of my new job and I hate being late, but what else can I do? Putting my phone away, I check the cage but Moe hasn't taken the bait. I'm going to have to do this the hard way. I lower myself onto my stomach and push myself underneath the bed. As I draw closer, my nose twitches at the pungent smell of cat urine, poo, and vomit. Oh. This is bad.

Training him to use the kitty litter was easy and he only had a few accidents in the early days. This situation isn't normal. I contemplate grabbing Moe by the scruff of his neck and dragging him out, but I'll drag the mess across the carpet. I want to keep it as central as possible. After a lot of faffing, I manage to rip my shirt off. I lay it in front of Moe, grab him by the scruff, place him on the shirt and drag him out that way.

When he's in the cage, locked and sitting on the table in the dining room, I go back and clean up the mess, change for work and search online for local vets. Finding one within walking distance, I ring them and they tell me to bring him straight in. I thank the receptionist, promising to be there within half an hour.

When I open the door to leave, cat cage in hand, I shriek in surprise.

"Mum?" My free hand flies up to my chest. "What are you doing here?"

Mum steps forward and kisses my cheek. "Sorry, I didn't mean to scare you, I wanted to surprise you, that's all." She glances at the cat cage and back up at me, brow furrowed. "Everything okay?"

"Moe's sick, I'm about to take him to the vet before I go to work." I shake my head, trying to make sense of Mum's visit. "You flew all the way from Adelaide to surprise me? There are no flights that arrive from Adelaide this early." I check the watch on my wrist. eight forty-five a.m.

"I arrived yesterday." Mum averts her gaze and clears her throat. "I didn't want to disturb you last night, so I stayed in a motel and thought I'd surprise you this morning before you started work."

Something is off, she's not herself. Her skin is pale, and her eyes are squinty. What is it with people hiding things? Jacques and now Mum? Why can't people say what they're thinking?

"How long are you here for?" I check the time again. Not even a minute has passed but I'm getting antsy. I need to go.

"I fly home on Saturday, so three more days. I won't bother you though, I've got the motel—"

"Don't be silly, you're more than welcome to stay. You know where the key safe is, the password hasn't changed. We'll catch up tonight, okay?"

Mum's shoulders slacken and she smiles. "How about I cook dinner?"

I grin and step out of my apartment. A night off from fast-food suits me. "That'll be great, thanks. Do you want to stay now, or will you come back? Jack's not back until Sunday so you'll have the place to yourself."

Mum takes a step to the side. "I'll stay and make myself a quick coffee then cancel my motel booking and do some shopping."

I nod, looking at her hard. "Are you okay?"

She steps through the door and into the apartment. "Of course, sweetie. I've got a bit of a headache, that's all. I'll take some painkillers shortly."

"Ah, okay. Well, rest up and help yourself to anything you need." I step up to her and give her a one-armed hug. The cage in my other hand wobbles as Moe moves and lets out a woeful meow. Mum hugs me back, her arms wrapping around me in her motherly way. I've missed her.

"It's so good to see you, Mum." I step back. "I'll see you after work."

I rush to the elevators and press the button until the doors open and I step inside. Too late, the doors close before I realise something.

Mum never gets headaches.

⟶⟩⟩ ⟨⟨⟵

This thought stays with me all the way to the vet and doesn't leave. Maybe I'm doing my overthinking act again, but this time I don't think so. Seriously, I don't remember a single time Mum has ever had a headache. She's one of those fortunate people. I don't take after her and I'm susceptible to them when I'm stressed.

This isn't normal for Mum.

It's after nine a.m. when I arrive at the vet surgery, and I'm seen straight away by a vet named Bella. She's a similar age to me, early thirties. She's short but petite with honey-blonde hair that hangs in a long ponytail down her back. When she smiles, her caramel eyes light up making them appear golden. I like her straight away.

"Jane, right?" she asks with a beaming smile, holding out her hand.

I take it and we shake. "Yes, thank you so much for seeing us." I hold up the cat cage where Moe releases another woeful meow.

Bella takes the cage and places it on the stainless-steel table, opening the door. She peers inside. "Hey there little one, what's making you so grouchy?" She reaches in and drags him out.

He meows louder this time and hisses. His fur is matted from sitting in his mess and my heart breaks for the little guy. I hope he's okay. What if it's my fault? I've never had a cat before, or any pet for that matter. I did some research on Google but what if it wasn't enough?

Folding my arms, I avert my gaze to the floor when unexpected tears sting my eyes. I draw in a slow breath, emotion washing over me. Not because of Moe, but I'm worried about Mum too. And Jacques, of course.

Two of the people I care most about are going through something and I hate not knowing. There's not a darn thing I can do and it's driving me insane.

"Hey, Jane?"

Blinking away the tears, I look up at Bella who's smiling.

"He's going to be okay."

Realising a stray tear is sliding down my cheek, I wipe it away and force a laugh. "Gosh, I'm an idiot. I've got a lot going on that's all." I shake my shoulders and breathe out a sigh. "I'm glad he'll be okay. Is it anything I did?"

"Probably not. Cats' stomachs can be very sensitive. Some cats will eat and drink anything without any problems. Others, like little Moe here, can have a little trouble. He's reacting to something that's disagreed with him. Do you give him cow's milk?"

I bite my lip and nod. "Only a little bit at night...oh I only started giving it to him recently. Could that be the problem?"

"It might be, not all cats can digest it because it's so high in lactose. Maybe try a lactose free one. Has he had his shots yet?"

"Shots?"

Bella rustles around in a drawer and removes a packet with a syringe. "Vaccinations."

"Oh," I rub my nose, "no, I didn't know he needed them."

"No worries." She smiles. "I can do that too. Now, didn't you say you had to get to work?"

I jerk to attention. "Uh, yeah of course. Is it okay to leave Moe here for the day?"

"More than, in fact I'd prefer to keep him overnight. Make sure he doesn't have any reactions to the shots, and I'll monitor him as I feed him cat-friendly food and milk."

I nod and run a hand through my hair, wincing when my fingers catch on some knots. "That's fine. I'll come by tomorrow after work, a bit after five?"

"Perfect."

I leave my contact details, give Moe a final pat then rush to work.

⟫⟫⟫ ⟪⟪⟪

"**W**hat time do you call this?" Regina demands when I walk into the shared office space. She stands from her desk, hands on her hips.

I stop short and glance around, the eyes of all my colleagues turning to me. I should remember their names by the third day but they're not sticking in my head. They're all nice enough, I suppose but keep to themselves. And since my job means I'm mostly by myself too, it's a little boring. I meant what I told Jacques, it takes six months to settle into a job. I must see this out.

"Uh, I sent you a text," I stammer.

"You were supposed to phone me, Jane." Regina tuts. "We went through this on day one. If you're late or unwell, you must phone the supervisor, AKA me. If you can't follow basic rules, what are you doing here?"

My mouth opens and closes a couple of times, words running around my head but not forming on my tongue. Everyone else has returned their attention to their computer screens but I know they're listening. "It won't happen again," I mumble, shuffling to my desk with burning cheeks.

After I log in, it's not even a minute later when an instant message pops up from Regina.

Let's do coffee tomorrow before work.

What the actual hell? I pound the keyboard as I type a reply.

What happened to you berating me 30 seconds ago?

An uncomfortable knot settles in my stomach as I question yet again whether I did the right thing taking this job. I wish I'd taken Jacques up on his offer. But what can I do? I'm trapped. Like I'm stuck in some kind of vortex...Cyclone Regina.

Oh that's gold. I bite back a giggle as I open my emails and check what jobs I've received. The distraction lessens the unease in my gut.

Until another message from Regina flashes on my screen.

It's all a front, darling. So, how does eight a.m. sound? Let's go to the same place we had lunch a couple of weeks ago.

Ugh. What's going on with her?

Can't do that early. Mum surprised me with a visit this morning and I'd like to have breakfast with her tomorrow.

I hear Regina's tut from here and I roll my eyes. Damn she's impatient. After a few messages back and forth we agree on ten a.m. tomorrow. I spend the rest of the morning working on the three emails I received.

When lunchtime comes, I eat my peanut butter sandwich on the go as I rush back to check on Mum only to find she's sleeping. Rather than bothering her, I go back to work.

A few more emails from sales come through during the afternoon, keeping me busy and out of Regina's way. She's a terminator in this new role and I'm not sure how I feel about it.

When the day ends, later than normal due to my late start, I go straight home to see Mum. It's seven p.m. and dark when I arrive at the apartment building. Residents are milling around the recreation area, enjoying the balmy evening. Kids are laughing and screaming as they jump into the pool.

The delicious scent of Mum's curry makes my stomach rumble when I enter my apartment a few minutes later.

"Something smells amazing." I close the door behind me. The apartment is warm from Mum's cooking but with a slight cool breeze from the open balcony doors.

Mum turns around from the stove and smiles. "It should be ready in about fifteen minutes. How's Moe?"

"He's going to be okay." I fill her in then go to change out of my clothes.

In my bedroom, I stop and stare out of the floor-to-ceiling windows. Taking my phone out of my trouser pocket, I check for any messages or missed calls from Jacques but there's nothing. He said he'd ring when he has lunch, which should be in a couple of hours, but I suppose I'd hoped to receive a good morning message or something.

He's got a lot going on, and he's busy, but I miss him so much. And now that Mum's here...

With a sigh, I change into shorts and a tank top and join Mum back in the kitchen. I set the table then we both sit down to lamb curry and papadums. We eat in silence for a few minutes but Mum only picks at her food.

"Mum, what's wrong?"

She avoids eye contact and shifts her curry around with her spoon. "Everything's fine." Her smile is forced. "Can't a mother spend time with her daughter?"

Losing my appetite, I put my spoon down and sigh. "Please don't do that. I never said you can't spend time with me, but you know as well as I do that you don't go anywhere without having a plan. Turning up on my doorstep without telling me first is unlike you. Did you and Dad have an argument or something?"

"What? No, don't be silly."

Mum and Dad don't often argue so it *is* a silly question. I shrug. "What else do you expect me to think? Why isn't he here?"

She sighs and puts her spoon down. "Don't worry about us, sweetie, everything is fine. He had things on so couldn't make it, but he knows I'm here. He's the one who suggested I visit..." she trails off and averts her gaze and if I wasn't already convinced she was hiding something, this would confirm it.

My stomach drops when it occurs to me. "The headache! You *never* get headaches, Mum. And that time at the markets, last time you were here, that was one too, wasn't it? It wasn't the sun in your eyes."

Guilt flashes across Mum's face, confirming my fears.

"C'mon, Mum. I'm sick of people not telling me things I deserve to know. Lay it out on the table, please."

Mum shrugs. "Alright, if you must know…" Tears build up in her eyes and she grabs a serviette, dabbing at them. "Jane, sweetie," she glances up at the ceiling and puffs out a breath, "I've got a brain tumour."

Chapter 15

Jacques

Dialling Jane's number, I hold the phone against my ear as I rush towards the cafe to meet Aimée. It is still surreal to think we are meeting after all this time. My mind is barely focused as I anticipate the conversation we will have.

Jane picks up on the second ring. "Jack, oh my gosh, I need to talk to you." Her voice hitches.

I am too highly strung, and her words don't register, they just wash over me. Remembering I never told her about meeting Aimée again, I say, "You will never believe who I am going to see."

The sun has made an appearance through the dark snow clouds. Is it a sign that I am getting closure on one part of my life? The anxiety of taking over Entreprises DuPont is missing today too. I am too excited about seeing Aimée again.

Does she have any idea how much of an influence she had on who I have become?

Jane sniffles and sighs. "Who?"

"Aimée."

I turn a corner and stop outside the café. It is lunchtime, so it is bustling, the outside tables taken up by patrons enjoying the unexpected sunshine. The heavy snow we had last night glimmers over the roads and pavements.

The café is on a corner, tacked on the end of two rows of Haussmann-style buildings going up two streets in a V shape.

"Your au pair from when you were a child?" Jane asks.

"Yes, she came into my office yesterday." I retell the story, aware that Aimée may already be inside.

"Jack, that's great," Jane says but her tone says otherwise.

I blink a couple of times but my attention is taken by a patron leaving the café and the sound of breaking glass from inside. It is a simple mishap, but my thoughts have been interrupted. My feet crunch on the snow as I move closer to peer inside the window, looking for Aimée.

In the recess of my mind, I remember Jane's tone. "Are you okay?" I turn away to avoid further distractions.

Her sigh is audible. "Yeah, all good. I had a busy day, I guess. Mum surprised me by turning up this morning."

My name is called, and I spin around, spotting Aimée poking her head out of the door and waving me over. I wave back and indicate I will be one moment. "Sorry, I must go. Enjoy her visit, she will be good company. I will call you back after lunch."

I hang up, pocket my phone and rush inside. Aimée smiles when I stop in front of her, reaching for my hands and squeezing them.

"It's so lovely to see you again, Jacques." She leans in to kiss my cheek and a waft of lavender reaches my nose, so like the scent I remember as a child.

Aimée gestures to a table against a wall. "Please sit, we have much to talk about."

Shoving my gloves in the pocket, I remove my jacket, hang it on the back of my chair and sit opposite Aimée. After we place and pay for our orders, we sit in awkward silence. Aimée will not make eye contact and is fiddling with a napkin, ripping it to shreds.

The burning question that has been on my mind since she left all those years ago fills the silence. "Why did you leave?" The childlike vulnerability is still there, and I glance away when Aimée looks at me.

"I was sick." Her hand reaches out to touch mine and I look at her. The half-shredded napkin sits in a neat pile in front of her. She moves her hand back and starts to shred the other half.

"I had a bad case of pneumonia and was in hospital for a few weeks. Your parents wanted me to recover before returning, but by the time I did I needed a change and that's when I went to Scotland." She drops the final shreds of the napkin and sits back with her gaze averted, folding her hands in her lap.

I stare at her hard, not buying the story. It may hold some truth, but I know my parents too well. Besides, Aimée will not meet my gaze so I am certain this is a story she has embellished.

The waiter delivers our coffees and I sit forward. "I was so young, Aimée." She meets my gaze, her light brown eyes shimmering with unshed tears. "You were sick, and I thought you had died. I was too young to think it could be anything else. Maman and Papa never told me anything else."

"I'm so sorry, Jacques, truly I am. But that's all I can say—"

"No!" It comes out forceful and Aimée's eyes widen.

I run my hands over my face before letting them fall into my lap. Anger is boiling deep within me, not at Aimée, but at my parents. She is withholding the truth for a reason, and maybe not of her own free will. For once I want the truth. I am sick of the games and the lies. I do not need the one person who I have idolised for many years doing the same.

"I am sorry, that was uncalled for," I say in a softer tone. "I only wish you would be truthful. I know my parents, and if you are not much changed from all those years ago, I am pretty sure I know you too. You taught me to always be truthful, and I had hoped you would pay me the same courtesy."

Aimée's gaze drifts to the front of the café and my own eyes follow. The sun has hidden behind clouds and tiny snowflakes are falling. People who had taken off hats, gloves, and scarves, have donned them again.

"I don't wish to lie," Aimée whispers.

Another waiter comes with our food and leaves again. Neither of us touch it.

"Tell me truthfully what happened," I beg. "How can it be so difficult?"

Aimée turns her focus back to me, frowning. "I signed a non-disclosure agreement. I wasn't allowed to talk about my time with you or contact you." She lowers her gaze and stares at her food. "They gave me money for my silence."

The air leaves my lungs, my world shifting on its axis. This should not surprise me, it is the sort of thing they would do, yet this is different somehow. A new kind of low. They knew how much Aimée meant to me. How much I changed because of her influence.

But that was the issue, was it not? While she looked after me, they lost control of me and did not like who I was becoming. I was not like *them*.

"I never touched the money," Aimée continues with a small smile. "I have not spent a single euro." She picks up a spoon and stirs her coffee even though she did not add sugar. "I would like to return it. To you."

I shake my head, holding my hands up. "No, I do not want it. It is money that does not belong to me. Money that represents my family, of which I do not want to be a part. Do what you want with it, donate it to a charity, put it towards a child's college...do you have children?"

"I have two daughters. My youngest, Sophie, is sixteen." She breaks out into a wistful smile. "She has Tavish's red hair and masses of curls. She did not want to move to Paris with Tavish and me, so she's still back in Scotland with Tavish's brother. My oldest, Avril, she is—" Her smile slips and her face pales. She shakes her head and shifts the cutlery around in front of her. "Never mind, you don't want to hear about my children." She forces a laugh. "Jacques, I am—"

"I do not mind hearing about them."

"Oh no, it's okay. I'm—"

"How old is she?" I am unsure why, but I have the urge to know. "Is she in university?"

Aimée deflates but there is fear in her eyes. "Jacques, please, I can't—I'm not allowed—"

I sit back in my chair and study her. "Not allowed? I do not under—"

My mouth snaps closed. The non-disclosure agreement. Is there something else she is not telling me?

"I'm sorry I never said goodbye or explained things," Aimee says. "I was so young and naive that I didn't think twice about signing the agreement. But when" she glances down at her coffee, running her finger along the handle, "—when they threatened to press charges if I returned, I was scared. It was partly why I left so quickly after I recovered."

"Partly?" My voice is a whisper. I have no idea what she is about to say and a sense of dread hangs over me.

"Jacques, if I tell you, I'll be breaking the agreement."

"They will never find out, at least not from me. You can trust me, Aimée."

Tears well up behind her eyes and she nods, sipping her coffee. There is silence between us while she thinks but I do not push her. I pick up my coffee, taking a long gulp, hoping it will calm me down. It does not work.

"I told you I had pneumonia, but I...I was also—"

She blinks a few times as she glances at the ceiling. "I was also pregnant," she finishes in a rush.

I stare at her nodding. She was young, in her early twenties when she looked after me and might have had a boyfriend.

Aimée appears frustrated as she runs her finger along the edge of her plate, the food still untouched.

"With your oldest daughter?" I coax.

Aimée nods and picks up a napkin from the middle of the table, dabbing at the corners of her eyes. "They were worried about me and the baby, so the doctors kept me in hospital longer. When I recovered and the baby was still developing normally, they discharged me."

"And you moved to Scotland right after?" I take another sip of coffee.

She nods again and scrunches the napkin in her hand, knuckles turning white. "Jacques," she huffs out a sigh, "my eldest daughter, Avril, is your half-sister." She buries her face in her hands, shoulders shaking with quiet sobs.

In the process of putting my coffee down, my arm jerks and I drop the half-full cup of coffee onto its saucer. Warm liquid splashes onto my hand and I curse, shaking it off. Reaching for a napkin, I wipe my hand dry while I stare at Aimée, my heart racing.

I have a half-sister? How is this possible? Papa and Aimée? No, surely not?

"It was a one-time thing." Aimée shakes her head. "I say one time but what I mean is it wasn't...consensual."

This time the world collapses beneath me. The words hang in the air and for a moment they do not register. One by one they slot into place. I remember his strange smile last night. He did not mention Aimée by name, but I am certain she is who he was referring to.

Mon Dieu. He was remembering.

My stomach rolls and nausea washes over me. The anger I have been trying to control bubbles upwards. I ball my hands into fists on my lap, focusing on breathing so I do not lose control, but it takes an enormous amount of effort. My dislike of my father turns to pure hatred. The thought of him doing *that* to Aimée...

I swallow hard and glance down at my half-drunk coffee and untouched food, losing my appetite. And my parents threatened to press charges if *she* returned? Or was it just Papa who made the threat? I may never find out, but knowing how much of a brute he is, it probably is him. Protect the DuPont name and all that.

So many thoughts go through my head. When did it happen? Why? I do not need the details...I do not *want* them, yet the questions are there. Perhaps not knowing would have been best. But I would not have learnt I have another sister.

The reality of it makes the warmth of the café too much. It is as though the walls are closing in on me.

I stand so fast my legs knock the chair, which falls back onto the hard wooden floor with a loud *crash*. The café falls silent, the eyes of all patrons looking at me. Eyes of people who would know who I am. If I thought the DuPont name was tainted once before, it is more so now. It is poisoned.

"Excuse me," I right the chair and grab my coat, "I need some air."

I rush outside. The snowflakes land on my face and I take large gulps of icy air as I put on my coat and gloves. My stomach rumbles, reminding me I have not eaten, but the idea of food is undesirable.

My father has always been a monster, but to do this...

I start walking with no destination in mind, but Aimée calls my name, running up and taking my hand to stop me. I am aware of coolness on my cheeks, but they are not snowflakes. They are tears.

This is too much. Maybe coming today was a bad idea.

"Jacques, I'm so sorry." Aimée comes around to stand in front of me, blocking the path. Her cheeks are streaked with tears, and I draw in a breath, reminding myself it is not about me. Aimée is the one who suffered, who went through horror at the hands of *my father*. I shudder at the thought.

I wipe my tears away with the sleeve of my coat and pull myself together. "I am sorry, it was rude of me to leave like that. I had no idea."

"Of course you didn't, you were only eleven years old."

Something occurs to me. "But you stayed after it happened. You would not have known you were pregnant straight away."

Aimée nodded. "Of course I stayed because I wanted to protect you from your family. When I got very sick and went to the doctor, I found out I was pregnant. That's when they put me in hospital and the rest is history."

Her words seep in, reducing my anger to a simmer but the hatred toward my father remains. Being angry will not fix anything, and I cannot do anything about it.

Oh, what I would do to have Jane here right now. I need her.

"Oh Jacques," Aimée reaches out to caress my cheek with her gloved hand, "if only I could have taken you with me. To take you away from that evil family of yours. I couldn't, but I have never stopped worrying about you. About what you might have become. To see you now, standing on your own two feet, out of their control," she holds a hand to her heart and smiles, "I am so happy."

I blink away my thoughts, her touch calming me. The way it always used to. She always had that way about her. Knew how to say and do the right things to calm me down when I was upset.

"I always remembered you," I confess. "Even though some of their ways seeped through, I tried to remember what you taught me. Then I met my girlfriend, Jane..."

I miss her like crazy and regret how quick I was to hang up when she needed me.

Aimée's eyes light up. "I would love to learn about her."

"And I will tell you, but first," I shake my head, still struggling to comprehend the news Aimée has given me, "my half-sister...Avril?"

Aimée nods and I realise that she is not just *my* half-sister. She is also Rémy and Céleste's half-sister.

"What is she like?" I ask.

Aimée's smile blossoms on her face, and she takes a step back. "She is much like you. Has your eyes and nose. Very placid and kind. She has a head for business, it must be in the genes." Her smile turns into a grimace.

"Why did you keep the baby?" I ask, aware it is a sensitive topic. "I would not have blamed you if—"

Aimée shakes her head. "It was not the baby's fault how she came about. Besides I could not bear to end an innocent life. I could give her the life she deserved."

"She has a wonderful mother."

I only wish I had a mother like Aimée. It is why she has meant so much to me, she was everything my mother was not.

Aimée's cheeks turn pink. "You're too sweet, Jacques. She has been told the truth about how she was conceived." She looks me in the eye when she adds, "And she knows about you and your siblings."

My breath catches. Will we ever meet? Do I want to meet her? I do not need to think about the answer. Of course I want to. She has had no connection to my dysfunctional family, she will be nothing like them. I imagine her being a mini Aimée, which warms my heart.

An icy breeze gusts down the street and Aimée shivers.

"Come," I offer her my elbow, "let us go back and finish our lunch. I am sorry for leaving so abruptly."

She loops her arm through mine and squeezes as we commence our walk back. "I understand, I told them we would be back so it will still be there waiting for us."

It is only a short walk back, but before we go inside, I ask, "Does Tavish know everything?"

Aimée nods. "He was the only one I could confide in. Being so far away in Scotland, I felt safe breaking the agreement. We met the very day I arrived as his family hired me as their housekeeper. Tavish was still living at home with his many siblings. We became instant friends and in time, more than that."

We go inside and return to our seats. My appetite has returned, and we start eating.

My mind drifts to Papa's will and how much everything is about to change. Although Aimée's confession has only proved one thing. Maman and Papa are nothing to me. Taking over Entreprises DuPont is not something I want to do, now more than ever before, but since I cannot get out of it, I only have two choices.

Merge it with my own company, bringing on their honest employees. It will not be considered selling, and since it is not doing well, it is the best option.

The second option is to convince Rémy to keep running it. This may take some work after our last meeting, but something deep down tells me that he needs this chance. He is not my father and deserves the opportunity to be trained. I will mentor him, but otherwise I will be nothing more than a necessary stakeholder and I will entrust all decisions to my brother.

If he does well, the company survives as does its employees and I will find a way to sign it over to him. Help him rename and rebrand if he wishes.

If he fails, I will merge it with my own company.

Either way, Entreprises DuPont will one day cease to exist, and it will bring me pleasure to make it happen.

Chapter 16

Jacques

Over lunch we talk about anything and everything, reacquainting ourselves as friends. No more bombshells are dropped. I have still not recovered from the last one. I will never forgive Papa. How am I supposed to look him in the eye when I see him next?

I have a half-sister. We share Papa's blood. I reflect on Papa's will and the clause mentioning 'all natural children of Marcel DuPont'. This cannot have been added on purpose, especially after everything he did to stop Aimée revealing the truth. Surely he would want to keep Avril a secret. Papa would not make that sort of mistake. Would he?

I still cannot come to terms with how evil Papa is.

In the end, Aimée agrees to keep the money he gave her. It is the least she deserves, but nothing will ever make up for the pain Papa inflicted on her.

The money will help to cover Sophie's university tuition, which she starts next year. It will also help Avril's business venture. I learnt she will soon be twenty-two years old and graduated from university late last year. She wishes to be an interior designer and run her own business. I do not know her, but I am proud.

Our conversation moves to Jane, and by the time I exit the café, I miss her more than ever. I need to talk to her. Tell her everything.

On the way back to the office, the snow is falling heavily, and the grey sky matches my sombre mood. I should be happy after seeing Aimée, but the bombshell has put a dampener on everything. Pulling the hood of my coat up, I power walk back to the office as the snow falls. We might get a blizzard. I have not checked the forecast, but I hope I am wrong. If we do, it will delay my flight home.

Removing my phone, I try to ring Jane as promised but it goes to voicemail. I frown and try again, but it does the same thing. It is unlike her to turn her phone off, especially since I told her I would call. Why now? Have I angered her that much?

I mutter a curse under my breath and type a text she can wake up to.

I am sorry I was distracted before. Please call me when you are free. I need to talk to you.

Je t'aime belle fille.

I press send but I can barely see the message through blurry eyes. My emotions are shot. I would do anything to hold Jane. I am only just hanging on by a thread.

Wednesday afternoon passes in a blur of one-on-one meetings with the staff. They are the last ones I have scheduled, but I am not as professional as I should be. I have been like a—how did

Jane word it once? —a bear with a sore head. It made me laugh at the time, but I am in no laughing mood right now.

They are experiencing me at my worst, and I am not proud of my performance. I always pride myself on not bringing my problems to work, but I have failed. When I walk through the office, staff look at me and talk behind their hands.

This is not the sort of office I had intended to run. I want to be approachable and transparent. I am far from either right now. I should not be here. I should have gone home after Aimée and I had lunch. I knew I was not in the right headspace.

"Hey," Claude comes into my office without knocking and sits in the chair opposite me, "what's with you today?"

I read the time on the computer. Four thirty p.m.

"I do not know what you mean," I say as I type a reply to an email.

"Yes you do." Claude lifts his feet and rests them on my desk.

"I would prefer if you did not do that," I chide, glaring at him.

He puts them down but has a triumphant smile on his face. "You're only proving my point. Usually you don't care."

Merde. I fell right into his trap.

"I do not want to talk about it." I send the email.

Well, I do want to talk but I would rather it be to Jane. No offence to Claude, he has always been a good friend, but will not help the same way Jane will.

Claude lifts his hands and gets to his feet. "Fine, no pressure, but I'm your mate first and foremost. If you need someone to talk to, I'm here." He goes to leave the office but then turns back. "Maybe you should take tomorrow off. You're not much good here, and I mean that kindly."

His smile is well-meaning. Sympathetic.

"I will, thank you, Claude."

"And come around for dinner tonight, okay? No arguments." He taps the door frame a couple of times and then leaves before I can argue because he knows me too well.

Sighing, I rub my temples. It is the least I can do to make up for my behaviour. I also owe my employees an apology. Before leaving for the day, I do so in an all-staff email.

When I leave the office, I go home to change before going to Claude and Penny's place. The memories of Jane are comforting. But *she* is not here.

I need her.

Even though she will be sleeping, I try to ring her once more but it goes to voicemail again. Unease settles in my stomach. Why has she gone quiet rather than talking things out? Were we not beyond this? Is there something missing that I do not understand?

Coming to Paris was supposed to be a quick effortless trip. It has been anything but.

Walking over to the floor-to-ceiling window, I glance out at the snow billowing past, a blanket of white covering the city. It matches my inner turmoils perfectly. With a sigh, I close the curtains then change into a clean set of clothes and leave for dinner.

Jane

I t's late, nearly midnight, but I can't sleep. Too much going on in my head. I tried to talk to Mum about the tumour, but she didn't want to. Said she had a bad headache and wanted to sleep it off with some painkillers. Of course I understood, but it meant I had no one to talk to. Not even Jacques. The one person who's usually there for me.

I've been sitting in my usual spot on the balcony overlooking the city and ocean since about nine thirty p.m. I finished my glass of red ages ago, but I can't bring myself to move to refill it. Too numb. Too shocked. Still unable to digest Mum's news. In the distance, a light from a buoy persistently flashes on and off. It's almost hypnotising.

Despite the occasional car, the city is in eerie silence apart from the whistle of the breeze through the palms and the gentle distant lapping of the water on the shore. A gust of wind catches strands of my hair and blows it into my face. I go to push them away, but they stick to my damp cheeks.

I wipe my tears away, along with my hair and draw in a breath of salty air.

Why did Jacques blow me off for his bloody *au pair* from when he was a kid? Like seriously! How can she be more important than me? I'm going through a crisis, Mum has a brain tumour, and he's not here when I need him.

Okay, so he said he'd call me back and I turned my phone off, that's on me. But he could've given me five minutes. Am I being unreasonable?

I so need to talk to him. He needs to tell me everything will be okay because I can't tell myself. I'm thinking worse case scenarios. Afraid Mum won't wake up in the morning.

Low-grade astrocytoma. Treatable but aggressive.

Aggressive.

I shudder at the word. She's going to need surgery, radiotherapy, and chemotherapy.

These are scary realities I never thought would apply to my family.

Because of its aggressiveness, it could progress to a higher grade if not caught in time. It's why she's here and why everything is happening so fast. She's seeing a neurosurgeon here that has experience in the surgery she needs.

How quickly can it change grades? Should I be worried? Is it terminal? All questions I needed to ask Mum but couldn't.

Maybe I should check on her, make sure she's breathing. What if it's already changed? Is that how it works?

Before rational thought can kick in, I stumble to my feet, ignoring the pain in my legs from being in the same position for too long. I tiptoe to the spare bedroom and press my ear to the door.

Silence.

I turn the handle and push it open a crack then I hear her soft breathing. I sigh in relief.

Shaking my head, I close the door and go out to the balcony to grab my glass. Time for a refill. Perhaps it'll help me gain some control and stop overthinking.

In the kitchen, I grab an open bottle of red from the wine rack as the intercom buzzes.

Jumping from fright, goosebumps rise on my skin and the hairs on the back of my neck stand on end. Who the hell is calling this late? Putting the bottle down on the counter, I press the button to answer. It doesn't have a camera, but it tells me it's from someone at reception. My racing heart starts to slow.

"Hello?"

"I'm sorry to bother you so late, Ms Collins," a man's voice says, "but there's someone here asking after you. She, uh," he clears his throat then adds in a whisper, "won't take no for an answer."

Who the hell could it be?

It occurs to me at the same moment a sultry voice over the line says, "Hey handsome if my friend isn't home, perhaps you'd like to take me home instead?"

Holy crap, it's Regina.

"I'm so sorry," I say, "I'll be right down."

I rush to my room to slide thongs on my feet, then I grab my key card and make my way downstairs.

I never told Regina my exact address, but I did let slip the apartment building we were living in once. And it was on the forms I filled in at work. I'm not surprised she found me. I'm more surprised she hasn't turned up before now.

When I enter the foyer, I spot Regina straight away. Dressed in a black mini dress, too-high heels, and her long red hair hanging in waves down her back, she's out for a good time. Leaning over the reception desk, her cleavage is in full view as she chats up a young, very hot but uncomfortable-looking receptionist. He's the only one working and must be the same one who called me.

I rush over to her and grab her arm. "Regina, what are you doing here?"

She straightens and turns, annoyance flashing across her features. It fades when she spots me. "Jane!" She comes in for an awkward hug.

Over her shoulder, I catch the receptionist's gaze and mouth 'sorry' to him. He shakes his head and smiles, telling me without words that it's fine even if there is obvious relief in his eyes.

"What are you doing here?" I pull away. "Do you realise how late it is?"

She adjusts the strap of her clutch on her shoulder and rolls her eyes. "It's not *that* late. Anyway," she holds up a bottle of red wine, "I was hoping I could hang around for a bit. I'm off to a club in about an hour, but don't want to wander the streets."

I sigh and nod, indicating with my head for her to follow me. It's not like I was going to sleep any time soon as it was. And I *was* about to have a refill, might as well enjoy it with her. I could do with someone to talk to.

"Bye, handsome," Regina says in a sickly-sweet voice, waggling her fingers in a wave to the receptionist.

We reach the elevators and Regina says, "A club nearby comes alive from about one o'clock." She flicks off an invisible spec on her dress. "I was hoping to hook up tonight, so I'll leave here about one."

I nod as the elevator doors slide open and we enter. Regina's lifestyle is so unlike mine, I have no idea what to say. I'm not one to judge, but I also don't understand the whole staying up late partying or hooking up with random strangers. I'm a one-man gal who likes to be in bed before midnight.

Jacques is my man, I don't want anyone else.

This thought settles in my mind and a calmness comes over me. Yes, he *is* my man. I glance at the promise ring on my finger. One day I hope it'll be an engagement ring. I must keep his promise at the forefront of my mind. I must believe that everything will be okay, and we'll work through these hard times together. It's just so difficult when he's so far away and we keep missing calls.

This means I also have to stop being immature and turn my phone on. How else are we going to talk otherwise? And he did promise to call me back.

Open communication, remember?

Honesty.

Don't keep things bottled up.

Right, got it.

Yes, okay, I was unreasonable earlier. It was a shock that he hung up so quickly when I needed to talk to him, but I know how much Aimée means to him. Seeing her again is a huge deal.

The elevator reaches my level and I step out with Regina following. Once she leaves, I'll turn my phone on and wait for his call. If I don't sleep tonight, so be it.

Chapter 17

Jane

I take two glasses of wine out to the balcony and hand one to Regina who's sitting with her legs stretched out in front of her.

"Thanks, darl." She takes it from me and guzzles half. "I hope you brought the bottle with you. I'm going to need a top-up soon." She grins.

I place my glass down and turn back to grab the bottle from the kitchen, plus the open one I left on the counter. We're going to need them. When I go back out onto the balcony, I close the door so we don't wake Mum.

Sitting in my usual chair, I place the bottles on the ground then pick up my glass and take a sip.

"Look at this view," Regina waves her arm to take in the view before us.

"It's pretty spectacular, huh?" I smile and tuck my legs under my bottom, the breeze warm and balmy on my skin.

"Yes, it is." Is that jealousy in Regina's tone? I turn to her, but her face is impassive.

"Is it normal for you to go clubbing on weeknights?" I ask, unable to help myself. "Will you be able to function tomorrow?"

Regina shrugs. "I'll be fine with lots of coffee. And no, I try not to go out much during the week. Remember the surfie hottie from the beach? Vince?"

I nod. How can I forget Regina's brazenness? That scene will forever be etched in my brain.

"He was a *hell* of a shag." She fans herself. "But he didn't want anything long-term, so I'm looking for the next best hottie. I'm a little...desperate, shall we say." She grins and waggles her eyebrows.

I shudder and shuffle in my seat. I'd rather not know the details of her sex life, thank you very much.

She guzzles the last of her wine then leans forward and refills her glass. She offers to refill mine but I've barely touched it, so I shake my head. I put the glass back on the table.

"So," Regina turns to me, "what's going on? You said your Mum was visiting? Was it a surprise visit?"

I nod and bite my lip, eyes filling up with tears. Drawing in a shaky breath, a tidal wave of emotion washing over me, I end up telling Regina everything.

Emotion overrides logic, and I can't control my tongue. Before I can stop myself, I'm ranting. About everything. Jacques going to Paris and my worry that he won't come back. Mum's diagnosis and upcoming surgery and treatment. Jacques not being here when I need him.

It all comes gushing out like floodwaters and by the time I'm done, tears are streaming down my cheeks. My wine remains untouched, whereas Regina has finished her second glass and polished off what's left in both bottles.

I glance across at her and she's staring at me with an unusual glint in her glassy eyes.

Oh hell.

I've just given her loads of ammunition. She's been so anti-Jacques and I don't like it one bit. Now that she's drunk, she could come out with anything.

Deep down, I know the things bothering me are normal relationship blips, especially since we're in a big transition settling in Australia. These feelings *must* be normal ... right? Either way, I should be talking to Jacques about this.

Not Regina.

But my phone is still in my pocket, switched off.

Geez. I've royally screwed up. Yet again. But it's not unfixable, I'm sure of it.

Regina gets to her feet, stumbling on her heels, and turns to me, placing one hand on the balcony for support.

"So, let me get this straight," she leans forward, reeking of wine, "Jacques couldn't even be there for you after such devastating news?"

I open my mouth to respond but Regina isn't done.

"He's manipulating you. You realise that, right?"

"No, he's not. You're drunk and talking nonsense."

"I may be drunk," she giggles and sways on her feet, "but I'm not *that* far gone. You're only proving my point. Everyone being manipulated denies it."

I stare her straight in the eye. "Just like you're manipulating me?"

Her eyes grow so wide it's almost comical. "Don't be lud...ludic..." she shakes her head, struggling with the word and settles with, "Don't be silly, you're my friend, I would never manipulate you."

I raise my eyebrows.

"It's true." She points a finger at me. "You're nothing more than a convenience to him."

I shake my head, refusing to believe it.

"Stop denying it, Jane!" Regina cries, her voice echoing off the walls. She waves her arms around wildly. "You need to listen to me. Are you listening?"

Not daring to speak, I just nod.

"I only have your best interests at heart, okay?"

She comes to crouch in front of me. When her mini dress rides up to show her underwear, I avert my gaze. This woman has no shame.

"I confess that I was a little suspicious of Jacques when I first met him," Regina says. "I mean why would a rich, popular guy like him follow you to Australia of all places? His life is in Paris where he can get anything he wants, any *woman* he wants, not second-rate Jane Collins."

"Alright, I've heard enough," I stand and sidestep the chair but accidentally knock Regina's shoulder. She falls back with a gasp but bursts out laughing.

To her, this is a huge joke, but the words play in my mind like a movie reel. I don't want to believe them, she's talking rubbish, but they're words I don't need to hear right now. I storm over to the door and am about to slide it open when Regina stops laughing and starts talking again.

"Wait, wait, I'm not done."

I turn back and take a step closer. "I am. I think you should leave."

Regina gets to her feet and stumbles over to me, grabbing my arm. "I mean no disrespect, Jane," she steamrolls ahead, not listening to me. "You're gorgeous in a plain sort of way, but you're not French. So, why did Jacques follow you all the way here? I've been thinking about it all this time, and it occurred to me. You said his family disowned him and this was his chance to start a new life and expand his company, but you do realise he's only using you, right?"

I stare at her, mouth gaping open. Regina's words seep in like poison. She's saying things I never once thought of...things that make a weird kind of sense.

Oh no. I shake my head, tears stinging my eyes. Why am I letting her get to me? Everything she says is untrue.

"Please. Leave." I repeat through clenched teeth, shaking my arm free from her grip.

"So, what are you going to do?" Regina glares at me.

I sigh and rub my temples. "About what?"

She rolls her eyes. "Jacques, of course. You can't keep going like this, Jane. It's unhealthy. He doesn't love you and I think you need to do yourself a favour and break up with him."

My mouth opens and closes wordlessly. I meant what I said before and she's proving it now, she is the manipulator here, not Jacques. She's been doing it since we met up. I turned a blind eye and now she's trying to tear us apart.

"You're jealous!" The thought coming to me. "That's what this is about, isn't it?"

Regina's eyes widen and her face turns a violent red, confirming my assumption even though she's shaking her head.

"Don't deny it. You're freaking jealous because I've got a great man who loves me. Who packed up his life for me to come here. Set up a business so we could stay here. And what are you? Just a miserable, sour woman who shags strangers to get off."

I've got no control over my words as the last day of pent-up frustration, worry and anger come bursting forth.

"I don't have to listen to this," Regina stumbles past me to the door and slides it open, juggling her clutch as she tries to place the handle over her shoulder.

"Don't forget, Regina," I keep my voice quiet so as not to wake Mum, "manipulators also deny being manipulators."

She turns to glare at me but she's shaking from anger. "I'm leaving."

"Go ahead, and you're not welcome here again. And for the record, I quit. Effective immediately."

She spins around so fast, she has to grab onto a dining chair to keep her balance. "You can't just quit!" she splutters, as though it's the most pressing thing.

"Yes, yes I can. The people I want in my life are already there and you're not one of them. Please leave now."

She stomps her foot before turning and leaving.

Once Regina has left, I lock the door, feeling lighter than I have in a long time. Tiredness overwhelms me and the only thing I can think about is sleep. I'll deal with everything else later.

⋙⋙ ⋘⋘

I jerk awake and sit upright in bed. I forgot to turn my phone on! Tiredly I glance around, groaning at the early morning sun shining through the gaps in the curtains. I reach for my phone on the bedside cupboard, but I can't find it. I shake my fuzzy head, trying to think where I might have put it. As I come to, I realise I'm still in yesterday's clothes and I pat my pockets until I find it.

Turning it on, I put it aside while I swing my legs around to sit on the edge of the bed, head in my hands. I go over everything that happened last night. I have no regrets about quitting. It was rash and I gave it no thought but it was right.

On the bed beside me, my phone vibrates with notifications. I don't check it straight away though. I need to get my head straight first.

After a few deep breaths, I let myself think. About everything.

I regret taking the job. There, I've said it. I've decided the whole 'six months are the hardest' is a load of rubbish. I mean, it *is* true...most times. But sometimes you're not the right fit for the job.

Last night showed me another side of Regina I don't like. Maybe I was tolerant of her before because I never saw her other side. Or maybe I didn't want to. Either way, I've changed a lot in the last eighteen months. I'm not the same Jane Collins and I don't need my old life, which is where Regina is from.

Why am I so determined to stay in Australia when it shouldn't matter where I go? I love it here, it's home and I'm close to Mum and Dad, but Paris isn't that bad. Not really. In fact, it's magical. Living there felt like a dream, and I think that was the problem. I never let myself settle because I always had my sights on returning to Australia.

But I *would* live in Paris for good if I had to. For Jacques. When he followed me to Australia, he said anywhere I was he would be. I would do the same. I know that now without a single shred of doubt.

The biggest spanner in the works is Mum's diagnosis. I want to be here, close enough to go back to Adelaide if she needs me. But Mum would never want me to put my life on hold for her. Besides she has Dad. I won't be able to do much, if anything.

Then there's the fact that I gravitate to everything in my old life. It's not something I think about, but it happens. This job for example. Same job. Same boss. All because it felt comfortable. Why didn't I tell Jacques I'd work for his company? I could've told Regina I changed my mind, but I wanted a job I was familiar with, with a boss I knew. Or thought I knew at least.

Now I wish I'd taken the risk.

Sitting up straight, I reach across for my phone and tap the screen. Seeing the text Jacques sent after his lunch break sends a wave of guilt over me. That would've come through while my phone was off.

Ugh.

Before replying, I send Regina an official resignation email. The last thing I want is for her to not remember what happened last night. I doubt it, but I'm not taking any chances. Three days in a job? That's a new record for me! Now I'm going to talk to Jacques and sort everything out.

I call him back, but it goes to voicemail, and I groan. This is all my fault.

Chapter 18

Jacques

S tanding on the balcony of Claude and Penny's two-storey apartment overlooking the Parisian suburbs, the cool air bites the skin on my cheeks and my breath comes out in visible puffs, like tiny clouds.

I still have not heard from Jane, and negative thoughts are crowding for space in my mind. Spiralling out of control. I cannot keep up the façade of being okay for long. My whole life is a lie, and I cannot move past this. It should not matter. I have been in this situation before when I was just a boy. But this time is different somehow.

I could talk to Claude, but he will not put my mind at ease the same way Jane does. She is aware of my deep-rooted fears of turning into my father. They are at the forefront of my mind tonight and I am terrified more than ever of it happening. I would never do what he did to Aimée, never in a million years, but what if he thought the same once upon a time?

Should I swear off ever having children? This is one thing Jane wants and once upon a time, I wanted them too...with her. Now I am not so sure. The only way to break the cycle of a toxic family is to put an end to the family name. I cannot speak for Rémy, but I maybe I should do my part.

If I do not have children I do not risk inflicting on them the same life I had. This may be extreme, but I cannot see any other way.

Merde. I rake a hand through my hair. *Jane, where are you?* I am clearly not in the right frame of mind to be thinking about this.

"Jacques, where are you?" Claude's voice from inside mimics my thoughts.

I turn around as the door slides open and Claude pokes his head out.

"There you are. Penny said dinner will be ready in ten minutes, but first Amélie wants *Oncle* Jacques to read her a story." He grins, knowing how much I love being called that.

A smile breaks free, and warmth starts in my chest, dousing the darkness for a short while. I smile and nod, stepping back inside to the warmth of their apartment, sliding the doors closed after me. Whenever I am here for dinner, which is at least once a week when I am in Paris, Amélie always wants me to read to her. I enjoy it and while my heart is not in it tonight, I will not deprive her.

On the way to her bedroom, I wonder if this is a sign that I am different. The fact that I want to make her happy rather than inflict any kind of misery on her. This is why I need to talk to Jane. She always says the right thing.

Amélie's door is ajar, and I knock on it before I go inside.

Amélie spots me and gasps, "*Oncle* Jacques," and grins as she jumps on her bed, making short work of settling under the covers.

She makes sure she is close to the edge and pats the space next to her with her little hand.

I sit next to her, back against the wall, and she snuggles into my side. "*Salut petit,*" I wrap my arm around her and stroke her hair. "*Qu'allons-nous lire ce soir?*" I ask her what we will be reading tonight.

Having not long turned two years of age, Amélie is still learning how to speak. She knows mainly French words but is learning English too. Strangely, she always wants me to read to her in English.

She holds out a book and babbles something in French, but her words are not clear. I take it from her and chuckle. It is a colourful book about Australian animals that Jane gave her before we left Paris last time. Not the sort of storybook Amélie usually chooses before bed, and it makes me wonder if she misses Jane as much as I do.

"Okay." I turn to the first page.

I read the animal's name and she repeats it after me while running her finger over the image, and then I read the description. This goes on for four more animals. When I move on to the fifth one, I read the name and she does not respond. I glance down to find her fast asleep. I smile and kiss the top of her head.

Penny comes in and goes to speak but her face softens. "Aww you two." Before I can protest, she whips out her phone and snaps a picture then comes over to help move Amélie without waking her while I get off the bed.

"Thanks, Jacques." Penny places a hand on my arm. "Come on, dinner's ready."

With Henri asleep before I arrived, and Amélie now sleeping, it is a quiet dinner with the three of us chatting about generalities. With my negative feelings temporarily silenced, I am more myself again. I miss Jane and I cannot wait to talk to her later, but I am in control. For now.

We finish eating at the same moment my phone rings. Hoping it is Jane, I excuse myself.

It is not Jane.

It is Maman. I open the balcony doors and step outside into the cool air.

"What is it?"

"Your Papa has taken a turn for the worst, Jacques. He has asked to see you. He does not have long left."

The line goes dead, and I pull the phone away, seeing she has hung up. Well. I should have expected nothing less. As the news sinks in, the control I had begins to slip away. My heart races and dread settles in the pit of my stomach.

I pocket my phone and go back inside to find Claude and Penny sitting at the table looking at me. While they know Papa is sick, I have not updated them on how things have evolved. Every time I think about it, it is not the right time.

Tonight, there is no time to explain so I say, "I am sorry, I must go. Thank you for a lovely dinner."

I go over and kiss Penny's cheek, clap Claude's shoulder and make my way to the front door before they can ask any questions.

"Wait a minute," Claude comes running up to me as I open the door.

I draw in a deep breath then turn to him.

"What's up, Jacques?" Claude asks behind me, concern lacing his voice.

Plastering on a smile, I turn to him. "Nothing. I am not feeling one hundred per cent I suppose. I will talk to you later."

Before he can say anything else, I turn and leave.

***

I am on autopilot and before I know it, I am at the hospital and walking towards Papa's room. When I reach it, my hand touches the handle and I stop, blinking a couple of times. What if this is the last time I ever see him? I must make it count, just in case.

Pushing down on the handle, I enter the room. Maman and my siblings are by his side. Papa is lying on his back, his breathing laboured and stilted. His skin is deathly ash.

The sight of my parents makes me sick. I never thought Papa could do something so disgusting. And Maman covered it up. Of course this is an assumption, but I cannot fathom how she would not know.

I make eye contact with Maman, Rémy, and Céleste before saying, "I would like some time alone."

They do not argue and vacate the room. With what I intend to reveal to Papa, I do not want them to hear.

I sit by his bedside, a heart monitor beeping next to it.

Papa must sense my presence as he stirs and turns his head to me, rasping in French, "Jacques. You are here."

"Yes, I am. Maman, Rémy, and Céleste are outside." I catch his dull gaze. "There are some things I must say."

Papa holds out a hand, but I do not take it. It falls to the blanket, a flash of hurt passing across his face.

"Me too," he says. "I am so happy you are here, I do not have long left to live. I needed to see you one last time." He moves his head back to the centre of the pillow, a lone tear sliding down his cheek.

I have never seen him cry. Ever. This is a surprising turn of events, but it may be a ruse to ease his conscience so he can die in peace.

"I have not been a good father to you," Papa's voice is raspy, "but I need to tell you that I love you and I am very proud of you and what you have achieved. I am sorry for the pain I have caused."

Unexpected tears prick my eyes and I blink them away. I will not fall apart by a declaration of love and an apology. When I needed to hear them as a child, he never said them. They are meaningless now.

If Papa made a miraculous recovery, he would be back to his old self in no time.

"Who are you apologising to?" I ask instead.

Papa blinks, appearing confused.

"To me? Céleste? Rémy?" I pause for effect. "Or to your other daughter?"

He gasps and then has a coughing fit. By the time he recovers himself, his breathing has worsened. Each breath sounds like a wheeze. "I have no idea what you are talking about," he whispers.

"Let me refresh your memory." I lean forward, so close I can smell the disgusting antiseptic on his ashen skin. "I know what you did to Aimée."

I sit back again, watching as his eyes widen and his face pales.

"I do not even want to know why, or how you could do it, but I want you to know this." I meet his gaze, full of fear but no remorse. Of course not. "You have destroyed our family and I will never, ever forgive you for that."

Papa gasps for breath.

"And one more thing," I add between clenched teeth. "Remember how your will states that 'all natural children of Marcel DuPont' will share a massive lump sum of money?"

He gasps again, his eyes full of panic. He tries to speak but his mouth only opens and closes wordlessly. Yes, it appears to have been an oversight. Even the mighty Marcel DuPont can make devastating mistakes. Now he is dying and cannot rectify it.

I rise and stand over him. "You should have specified which children the money should go to," I say with a triumphant, bitter smile. "But do not worry, I will make sure all four children have their share. We do not want anyone missing out, do we?"

He gasps again but this time it sounds like he is choking. The machine next to him starts beeping frantically. Papa keeps gasping and clutching at his throat, but no air is going in. The door bursts open, and nurses rush in shouting orders. I am pushed back out of the way, watching on emotionlessly while they try but fail to revive him.

Maman and my siblings come in, standing next to me. Maman is sobbing but my siblings are wearing similar emotionless expressions.

Papa takes his last breath as the machine flatlines next to him.

Maman breaks down and falls into Céleste's arms. I glance at Rémy whose eyes are shining with tears but neither of us speaks. I leave the room without a backwards glance.

On the way to my car, the relief of his death is instantaneous. The first call I make is to Aimée. It is not too late yet, and she answers on the first ring.

"Jacques?" She sounds surprised to hear from me. "Are you okay?"

"Papa is dead!" I declare, sounding far too excited for what should be terrible news.

"What?" Her sigh is audible through the phone. "Jacques, I'm so sorry."

"I am not! After all the grief he has caused me...and *you*. Aimée, do you not understand? You are free of him."

There is silence and the soft sound of crying.

I do not feel the cold air on my skin as I exit the hospital and approach my car. Once I have finished talking to Aimée, I will ring Jane and tell her the news. Everything is looking up.

"And that is not all." I press the fob to unlock my car, proceeding to tell her about the will, including the money Avril will be entitled to.

"Jacques!" Aimée sounds horrified. "No, I want nothing to do with that!"

"It is for Avril, not you."

"No, Jacques." Her words are angry, and I fumble with the car door handle. "Don't you realise what this will do?"

I open the door and slide into the car, my excitement petering out. "What am I missing?"

"The non-disclosure! If it gets out Avril is his, I could be sued!"

"No, that will not happen." As I speak the words though, I am uncertain. I must dig deeper into this. With what Aimée went through, surely it cannot be enforceable?

This conversation is not going the way I envisaged. I think quickly before continuing, "It will never have to be revealed who the mother is, I will only need to talk to Avril—"

"No!" Her voice is shrill, panicked. "Did you ever think about what *she* wants, Jacques? She does not want anything from her father. Especially not his money."

"Should she not have a say in this?" The words are out before I can stop them.

Aimée's sigh is audible. I have pushed her too far. Her next words shatter my world into a million tiny pieces.

"It was a mistake making contact again. Leave it alone, Jacques. Leave *us* alone, please. I will ask Tavish to handle our business affairs, but otherwise we want nothing to do with you or your family."

And just like that she is gone from my life again. But this time it is my fault. It was stupid to bring it up, to think that offering Papa's inheritance would fix anything. The DuPont name and the tainted money will only ever bring heartbreak. The fact she did not want the money Papa originally gave her is telling enough.

The fears I have been struggling to control return with force. Aimée did not say the words, but she has proven that my family name will forever be tainted. How can I ever share this with anyone?

The simple truth is...I cannot.

Chapter 19

Jacques

I sit in the car, my hands gripping the steering wheel so tight my knuckles turn white. The hum of the idling motor and the air from the heater are the only sounds. Millions of thoughts are crowding for space in my mind. I was on such a euphoric high minutes ago, but now it is as though it never happened. Those dark, negative thoughts come back with force. There is no controlling them this time.

My phone starts vibrating in my pocket and my heart skips. Removing it, I see Jane's name flashing on the screen. At last. I go to swipe the screen but stop.

With Jane, I am the happiest I have ever been. She has shown me what life could have been like.

Could.

One word that changes everything.

It is not just because of Aimée's reaction, although that is at the forefront of my mind. But Papa's death has hit me hard. I am all too aware of what I have missed out on. He was never the father I needed, and I will never have another.

Who was I fooling? I am a broken man because of him. I will never escape the cursed and tainted DuPont name. How can I inflict this life on Jane?

The call rings out and I place the phone on the dashboard.

Even with Papa gone, the stigma will remain. Maman is still alive and the last few weeks have only proven she will always be there. I will never be able to cut her off, especially when I take over Entreprises DuPont.

If Rémy changes his mind about taking control, and if he is successful, the business will continue to grow and thrive. I cannot in my right mind merge it with mine without first giving my brother a chance to prove himself without Papa's influence. That means I will forever be connected to it.

With a heavy heart, I pick up my phone and call Jane back.

She answers on the first ring. "Jack! I'm sorry. I'm so, *so* sorry."

Hearing Jane's voice should make everything right...but it does not. If anything, it only tears at my heart knowing what I must do. *For her.* A lone tear trickles down my cheek, followed by another.

"I was stupid, and selfish, and upset over a petty thing," Jane rambles, unaware of my turmoils, "but I shouldn't have turned my phone off. I miss you, and I wanted to talk to you, but we kept missing each other, and—"

My tears are relentless now and a strange sobbing noise sounds from the back of my throat.

A pause, then, "Jack?" Jane sounds concerned.

I draw in a shuddering breath and wipe my tears, which only makes way for more. It is as though something inside me has broken and now all I feel is emptiness and hatred. *So* much hatred towards Papa.

I will never get closure. I will never have a father. I will forever be burdened by this life. I never asked for this. I did everything in my power to escape it. Now I have gone full circle and ended up where I never wanted to be.

I am aware of Jane asking me if I am okay, but I cannot form words. The last time I cried like this, the type where the tears do not stop and your soul is being ripped out of you, was after Aimée left. Maman caught me and said only weak children cried and told me never to do it again.

I did not for a long time.

On rare occasions I have shown emotions in front of Jane, like now. I can be myself. But it is still unnatural. I feel so vulnerable...so weak.

Now I am crying after losing Aimée a second time. Mentioning the inheritance to her was a stupid, *stupid* idea.

Saying it to Papa was one thing, but following through with it? Terrible idea and now I have lost two people. One I cared about, one I did not. And now I am about to lose a third...who I love more than life itself.

I never wanted to lose the future I set for Jane and me. I vowed to never let my family come between us. But I have failed at both. How can I let her into my life now? I cannot bestow that stigma on her. I must let her go.

"Jack," Jane's concerned voice penetrates the fog, "please talk to me. What's wrong? Is it about last night? Because I'm so sorry."

I shake my head even though she cannot see me. If only that was the only problem here, I would not be in this mess. Jane does not need me like this. She needs someone strong and dependable. The person I used to be.

I fear I never will be him again.

"I cannot do this," I mumble, my voice not sounding like my own.

The last thing I want to do is hurt Jane, but she must realise this is for the best.

"Papa died tonight," I add, my voice hitching around the words. I hate it. Why must I feel anything?

"Oh, Jack, I'm—"

"Do not be sorry." My tone comes out angrier than I intend, and I draw in a deep breath to calm myself. "This is the least he deserves." I pause, thinking. "I found some things out before his death. It...changes things."

"Okay," she says, "like what? Whatever it is, I'm sure we can work through it together."

I laugh despite myself. It sounds bitter to my own ears. "No, I do not think we can."

"What do you mean?" Jane's voice wobbles.

"I will not be returning to Australia," I say, forcing the words out. "Hayden will continue running the business and I will support him online from here."

I have not given this any thought at all. All I know is I need to set Jane free. She should not be associated with a family like mine. It is bad enough I tried to do it to Aimée, I will not do it to Jane.

"Why?" Jane's voice is a whisper, her breathing laboured. "No, Jack, please don't do this. It's not as bad as that. There's so much we haven't talked about."

"I am sorry, but none of that matters now. This is how it must be."

"Jack, you can't do this!" Jane sounds hysterical. "You promised, remember? You gave me a ring and you promised!"

I close my eyes and will the pain to go away but it only intensifies. I swallow the lump in my throat, forcing the next words out. "Goodbye, Jane."

Her sobbing protests as I hang up will haunt me forever. I rest my head on the steering wheel, hitting the horn, which blares into the night. My chest is tight, as though it is about to burst.

What have I done?

The right thing, that is what. I have done the right thing.

Turning my phone off, probably for the first time ever, I pocket it and pull myself together. When I drive away, rather than going home, I go to the DuPont office instead. I park the car and go to stand in front of it, staring at the large multistorey building. To think this will soon be mine. The idea fills me with dread.

"I should have guessed you would be here."

I turn in alarm to find my brother standing next to me, hands dug deep in his smart trouser pockets, shoulders hunched, skin pale.

"Congratulating yourself, are you?" he adds, continuing in English. "Do you not have everything already? Why do you need this?" He gestures to the building.

It is going to be difficult to get Rémy to listen, but he might be more willing tonight. I contemplate how much to tell him, still not knowing if he can be trusted. I have sympathy for him, but I must tread carefully.

"No, Rémy," I say, my heart aching after the call I just made, "I have lost everything."

Rémy's eyebrows knit together, an unspoken question in his eyes. I must look a sight after my breakdown. I lower my gaze in a fruitless attempt to hide the evidence.

I clear my throat. "Why are *you* here?"

"I suppose I hoped to find some answers."

I glance back at him, taking in the bags under his eyes and the sadness in them. His gaze meets mine.

"I might be able to help." He appears sceptical so I add, "I have no reason to hurt you, Rémy. I have just given up the woman I love and my life in Australia because I do not want to inflict this life on her. Now I have an opportunity to be the brother I never was. I hope you will let me."

Rémy stares at me for a long moment, confusion creasing his brow. Then realisation dawns on his face. "You are an," he pauses as he contemplates a word, "*espèce d'imbécile*, whatever that is in English."

I laugh and some of the heaviness between us dissipates. "Idiot is the word you are looking for, and yes I know I am."

Rémy shakes his head in disbelief and inclines it to the door, a tiny flicker of a smile kicking up the corners of his mouth. "Papa has a secret stash of cognac in his office. Would you like to share a drink in his memory?"

"I will drink to his death, but not to his life."

Rémy smiles a little easier this time and he nods. Removing his security card, he swipes us in, and we take the elevator to the top floor.

Entering his office, Rémy goes to the desk in search of the alcohol, while my gaze is drawn to the view outside the floor-to-ceiling windows. Light streams through the windows over the furniture. The snow has stopped, but the city is still a blanket of white. More snow is forecast and flights in and out of the city are continuing to be cancelled.

Memories of Jane try to return but I force them away and join Rémy at the desk where he has placed a full crystal decanter of cognac and two matching glasses. Rémy sits in Papa's chair like he is used to it until I remember he *has* been acting in this role for many months now.

I sit opposite and accept a glass.

"To his death." Rémy raises his glass.

"To his death," I repeat, leaning forward to clink glasses.

The first sip of the reddish-brown liquid slides down my throat. I do not care how much I drink tonight. I will find another way home if I must.

We sip in silence, and my gaze is drawn to the window once more when snowflakes start drifting past it.

"Alright *grand frère*," Rémy says, "tell me why you hate Papa so much. Is this not what family is supposed to do when someone dies? Talk about their life?"

"Where are Maman and Céleste then?"

Rémy chuckles coldly. "Celebrating I presume." He sips his spirit and glances at me over the glass.

We talk and drink for many hours. We savour the alcohol, not getting blind drunk, but drinking enough to loosen up. Rémy and I talk like we have never done before. All my assumptions about him have been correct. Being the unwanted and forgotten child, he was shipped away and only offered the company as an afterthought when I refused. He has been treated badly and it hardens my resolve to give him a chance.

"Were you serious yesterday about letting me continue running Entreprises DuPont?" Rémy asks in the early hours of the morning when the sky starts changing colour.

I hold his gaze when I nod. "Yes, I was...I *am*."

"Then I accept your offer."

I sigh in relief and polish off my glass. This time I do not refill it. My body is buzzing and the constant pain in my chest has been numbed. It is enough. For now.

"We have much to talk about." Rémy finishes his glass and refills it. When he offers to refill mine, I shake my head.

"No lies, excuses, or manipulation. Got it?" Rémy adds.

I glare at him deadpan. "If I pride myself on anything, it is not being like the rest of my family." Rémy scowls and I add, "I cannot compare myself to you. I never got to know you."

We certainly have a long way to go, but I think we are on the same page. We stare at each other, a strange surge passing between us, drawing us together as brothers. There is so much we do not know about each other, so many misunderstandings and lies, but it is all changing.

I have seen firsthand how a death in the family can either draw a family together or further apart. A divide has already formed, but I have an opportunity to connect with my baby brother.

Rémy looks at me curiously. "If that is what you pride yourself on, why did you give up your life?"

I stare at him, the question catching me off guard.

"It was the right thing," I say and move the conversation onto business.

Anything to keep it away from the truth.

⁓≫⟩ ⟨≪⁓

Jane

Lying face down on the bed, I sob and sob and sob into my pillow, hoping like hell Mum doesn't hear me. She doesn't need to see me like this.

Pull it together. Come on, you've got your Mum to worry about.

Except the internal voice does nothing but make me cry more. I've lost Jacques now I might lose Mum.

There's a gentle tap at the door, followed by, "Jane, are you okay?" from Mum.

Damn it!

I lift my head for air then bury my face again, holding in my sobs but my body is shaking, betraying me. When the door opens, I know I've failed to hide this from Mum.

"Jane, sweetie, what's wrong?" The bed dips and Mum starts stroking my hair.

I can't hold in the sobs and they come bursting out. I force myself to sit up and collapse into Mum's arms. She holds me tight, continuing to stroke my hair as she rocks me back and forth.

"I'm sorry," I say between sobs.

"Shh." Mum squeezes me and kisses the top of my head. "Don't be sorry."

"B-but you're going through—" I can't finish the sentence, the thought of Mum's tumour making me cry even harder.

"It's okay," Mum whispers, "everything's going to be okay."

Is it? I can't even comprehend what's going on. Nothing makes sense. Why is he doing this? Give up everything he's worked so hard for? Was Regina right after all? Has he been using me this entire time?

No, don't go there.

What the hell am I going to do? How can I stay here if Jacques and I are over?

Just the thought sends me into fresh sobs.

Too much crying makes my head hurt. I need to pull myself together.

Drawing in a couple of shuddering breaths, I pull away and push my soaked hair away from my face. Mum reaches for a box of tissues on my bedside cupboard and holds them out. I grab a handful and wipe away my tears. It's hard to make them stop, but they do, and I grab a couple more to blow my nose.

"Are you ready to talk about it?" Mum's worried gaze holds mine.

I can tell she has a headache by the look in her eyes.

"Have you taken your pills this morning?" I ask instead. "I'm the least of your worries right now."

She purses her lips and shakes her head. "Helping you keeps my mind off it. I'll take pills with some food soon. Now, come on, tell me what's going on."

No one told me a breakup could hurt this bad. When we broke up in Paris it was tough, but we'd only been together a few short weeks.

This time...we've been together for over a year. It's a *lot* different.

Tears threaten to fall again, two dripping down my cheeks and I grab another tissue, willing them to stop.

I draw in a breath and blurt, "Jack broke up with me."

Mum recoils. "What? Why?"

I shrug and place my used tissues on the bed next to me. "I have no idea! He just said he couldn't do it anymore, that something had happened and that was that. He even gave me a promise ring, Mum." I hold up my hand, fresh tears brimming my eyes. "He promised we'd work through anything together. Why did he break that?"

Mum's mouth opens and closes but she doesn't speak. "Has anything led up to this?" she asks after a few beats.

"Marcel, his father, died—" I work my jaw and wince in shame. "They had a pretty toxic relationship. I guess it affected him more than he expected."

Mum takes my hand in both of hers. "Everyone reacts differently to grief and it's unavoidable, even if they had a bad relationship."

"I understand that, but to break up with me? C'mon, Mum, that's a bit extreme, isn't it?"

She shrugs one shoulder and lets my hand go, sitting back, "Perhaps, unless something else happened?"

I huff out a sigh and scrub my hands over my face. "He saw Aimée the other day."

"Who's that?"

I explain the connection and then add, "But she's a good person from his past, someone he's looked up to. I can't see that being an issue. Our relationship was a little tense this week because we kept missing each other, but it wasn't anything we couldn't work through." I groan and cover my face with my hands. "It took us ages to talk and when we did this morning, this is what happened."

Mum offers a sympathetic smile. "I know how difficult this is Jane, but it's a simple solution."

"Simple? Really?" I stare at her in awe, hoping she's got some life-changing advice to give me.

She nods then leans over and takes my face in her hands. "Give him some time, Jane. It's not easy when you want to support him but he needs this time. Maybe check in with his business partner. Claude, is it?"

I nod.

"Check in with him in a day or two, I'm sure he'll put your mind at ease. But for now, let Jack do things his way, okay?"

"Ugh." I flop onto the bed and hold the back of my hand to my forehead. "And here I was thinking you could fix it."

Mum chuckles and gets to her feet. "That I can't do, but I *can* help you keep your mind off things. How about some breakfast and I'll take my pills, then when my headache has eased, we can do some shopping."

I sit up. "But you need to rest."

"Don't worry about me." She leans down and takes my hand, tugging me so I have no choice but to stand. "I'll be okay in a bit."

She frowns and then glances at the digital clock on my bedside table that reads seven thirty a.m. "You're working today, aren't you?"

I grab my sodden tissues and smile sheepishly at Mum. "Yeah, about that...I'll fill you in over brekky."

Chapter 20

Jane

I'm going to miss these sunrises.

It's Friday morning and once again, I can't sleep. Last night I managed three hours and gave up at five a.m., resuming my normal spot on the balcony to watch the sun rise.

I miss Jacques.

I'm worried about Mum.

I'm trying to figure out what to do.

Reaching across for my coffee, I take a sip and hold the mug between both hands. The sky is covered in light clouds, the horizon a mixture of pinks, purples, and blues. When the golden orb of the sun peeks above the horizon, the clouds are lined in gold and rays of light spread across the sky in an arc. The still ocean mirrors the image perfectly.

Yes, I'm *really* going to miss these sunrises because it's pretty clear what I have to do. I've got to leave. I can't stay here without Jacques. I *definitely* can't afford the rent. I'm going to have to go back and live with Mum and Dad.

Who would've thought that thirty-two-year-old me would end up going back to live with Mummy and Daddy because I can't keep my life on track?

Not me, that's for sure.

Yeah, I love Mum and Dad, and they're easy to live with, but I'm supposed to have my life together and a couple of kids by now.

Where did it all go wrong?

There's a soft meow from the doorway and seconds later Moe jumps up on my lap. I put my coffee back on the table and pat his small head. I'm so glad he's okay. I picked him up from the vet's last night and he was back to his normal self. Bella the vet put him on a strict lactose-free diet and he's back to skidding around the apartment at lightning speed.

"What am I going to do with you?" I scratch him under the chin.

He meows at me and blinks as though that's supposed to solve everything.

"Nope, that doesn't help. Guess I'll have to give you up too."

As I say it, my heart breaks in two. I've grown to love this little fluffball and I don't want to give up on him. Moe sits on my lap and judges me with those green eyes. He meows again but he's not purring. Does he understand me? It sounds silly but he might...

"Stop looking at me like that," I scold. "What do you suggest I do, huh?"

He stands on his hind legs, placing his two front paws on my chest. I lower my face and he butts his against mine and starts purring. How can I ever give him up? Is it so wrong to keep him? He's not a *thing*, he's an animal that needs care and attention.

I need other solutions. I just need time to think. Moe deserves a loving home and at least that's something I *can* do. I'll ask Mum and Dad if I can bring him home with me. It won't be for long.

I run my hand across his soft fur, from his head, across his back and to the end of his tail. "Alright, you win. I'll see what I can do."

He meows quietly and I *swear* he smiles at me in a cat-like way. He curls up on my lap and falls asleep.

Grabbing my coffee, I finish it off and place the empty mug back on the table. Guess my focus today should be on packing my things. I can't in my right mind stay here. The lease agreement might be in joint names, but Jacques is paying the rent. It would be wrong to take advantage of that. I refuse to use Jacques' money even if we do have a joint account. It's not right, and I'm not the type of person to steal money out of spite. Tempting though it may be. I've got enough in savings to tide me by for a short while, but I'll need to find another job. Fast.

Ugh. This is what happens when I'm between jobs and become too reliant on Jacques.

Jacques.

This whole thing is a mess. I haven't heard from him since our last call yesterday. Not. A. Single. Word. Even Claude and Penny have gone quiet. It's like I've dropped off the face of the earth. Well, *their* earth at least. I bet they're rallying around Jacques, giving him the support he needs while leaving me to lick my wounds.

Then again, *I* haven't tried to contact them either, so it's not a fair assumption.

I pick Moe up and transfer him to the other chair, and then I stand and take my mug inside. It's nearing six thirty a.m. and I want to surprise Mum with breakfast in bed. Besides, she'll be due her pain medication soon and it always works better with food. I may not cook very well, but I *can* manage edible scrambled eggs.

Placing my mug in the sink, I glance around the apartment with a heavy heart. Should I pack up our things? I can't store them anywhere, but I should make a start I suppose. Bitterness seeps through my veins as I consider packing my things and leaving everything else for Jacques to deal with. After all, *he* dumped *me*. It's only fair he sorts it out, right?

But I'm not that nasty.

I can at least pack everything up, that's better than nothing. I suppose it's best to start in the hardest place.

The bedroom.

But first, breakfast.

I take the ingredients out of the fridge for the eggs when Mum appears from the bedroom, shuffling along the floor, eyes squinted. She mumbles a good morning before settling down at the table, cradling her head in her hands. I hate seeing her like this. She's always so strong and never complains about a single thing. Even the flu can't keep her down for long.

"I was going to bring breakfast to you," I keep my voice low. "I assume you've taken your pills?"

Mum lifts her head with a tight smile, managing a small nod. "Thanks, sweetie. Just something light though, I'm a little queasy from the headache."

I nod and put some toast in, one slice for Mum and two for me. While the pan heats, I crack eggs into a bowl for the scramble.

"I've got an appointment with the surgeon this afternoon," Mum says. "Would you like to come along?"

I glance up while I whisk the eggs, nodding without hesitation. I'd like to hear what they have to say.

"Good," Mum says.

I pour the eggs into the pan. "I think it's great he's travelling to Adelaide to do the surgery, it means Dad can look after you. How's he taking it, by the way?"

I'm glad Mum's talking more about the tumour. Over the last couple of days, she's been very quiet about it and when I've asked questions, I only received one-word answers.

Mum's smile is sad. "He was a mess at first, but you know what he's like. He goes into practical mode and starts gardening."

I chuckle. Gardening, yes, Dad's favourite pastime. I used to wonder why he never did it as a job, he'd make a brilliant designer. But he always said he didn't want to make something he enjoyed into a career. I guess I understand that and I'm glad he has something to keep him busy.

"The surgeon said he'd also come to Adelaide for all my appointments, as he has other patients there," Mum adds. "But your father thought it'd be a good idea to do two of my appointments here so I could spend some time with you. Honestly, I think he just wanted me out of the house because I'll worry more about him than my health."

I smile and stir the eggs while waiting for the toast to pop. Once it does, I butter it, finish cooking the eggs and divide it between the two plates, taking one over to Mum. I go back for cutlery and seasoning then sit in front of her.

"Thanks, sweetie." Mum picks up her cutlery.

As we eat, Mum perks up when the pain medication starts to work. She takes her time eating, moving bits of toast and egg around her plate. I can tell she's losing her appetite and worry grows in my gut. Is that a symptom of cancer?

"Mum," I say when I've finished eating, "I may have to move back in with you and Dad, will that be okay?"

She looks up in surprise.

"It'll only be for a short while, until I find another job," I add.

"Jane," she reaches across for my hand and squeezes it, "you know you're welcome home any time, but aren't you being a bit rash?"

I stare at her, shrugging. Am I? Moving out is the right thing to do, surely.

"Remember yesterday I said to give Jack time."

I nod and place my knife and fork across my plate. "It's not right to stay here, Mum. He's broken up with me, and hasn't made any contact, I must do the right thing."

"Must you?"

"Mum! You were always the one teaching me about doing the right thing."

She chuckles and sits back in her chair, done with eating. She only ate half of her eggs and toast.

"And I stand by that, but this is different. I'm not convinced this is it for you two."

A seed of hope buries itself in my gut. "You're not?"

She shakes her head. "Every relationship has its blips." She glances at the clock on the wall and gets to her feet. "I'll shower and change then we should leave about eight-thirty. My appointment is at nine."

While Mum is doing that, I tidy up the kitchen, thinking over what she said. Dare I hope that this isn't the end?

❦

After Mum's appointment, she goes straight home to rest but I spend some time at the beach. Just walking the shore, the sand massaging the soles of my feet, the warm breeze caressing my skin. Thinking.

I was glad to hear firsthand from the surgeon about Mum's condition and what was being done. But he was so serious. Everything happened so fast. Before I knew it, her surgery was booked for two weeks' time, making everything so real. He even put her on a waitlist in case anyone cancelled. They weren't taking any risks.

He said he couldn't promise anything but he was positive and upbeat, confident that he could successfully remove the tumour. The positivity put my mind at ease a little. There's still so much uncertainty though. Removing the tumour doesn't mean a miraculous recovery.

Stopping at the spot where Jacques gave me the promise ring, I sit on the sand and transport myself back to that night.

The hope of our future. The complete trust I had in him. Still do.

Maybe I *am* being too rash wanting to pack up the apartment? My phone rings, interrupting my thoughts. Removing it from my pocket, I answer it.

"Is that Jane?" a male voice asks.

"Yes, who's speaking?" I settle on the sand, legs outstretched.

"It's Hayden Ashcroft, Jacques hired me as the Regional Manager of Executive Solutions. He gave me your number in the off chance I couldn't contact him."

My heart stops and my breath catches in my throat. "You can't reach him?"

"I know, right? It goes straight to voicemail. I've never had any problems reaching him before. He answers regardless of the time. I swear that dude never sleeps."

Hayden laughs like it's nothing, but warning bells are going off in my head.

Jacques never turns his phone off. *Ever.* Tears well up in my eyes but I force them back. I'm not about to start sobbing to the new Regional Manager.

The bigger issue here is the fact Jacques has his phone off. On the occasions that he does, it's while we're sleeping, but that's rare. It's one thing he's never changed. He takes his job seriously and I love him for it.

A tear slides down my cheek but I don't wipe it away.

Jacques turning his phone off.

His admission that he won't be coming home.

Not giving a second thought to the Australian office. The thing he's worked so hard for.

Giving up on *us.*

Jacques doesn't break promises. He's one to go all out to keep them. Like how he did so we could stay in Australia.

He doesn't just *give up.* Things start slotting into place.

Maybe Mum's right. Jacques is grieving his father in his own way, but what the hell am I doing letting him tackle it on his own? I should be there. If he doesn't need me right away, fine, but at least I'll be in the same country when the time comes that he does.

I should *not* be on the other side of the world.

"Uh, Jane?" Hayden's voice interrupts my thoughts. "Are you there?"

I suck in a breath of air and ignore the pain in my chest, focusing on the present. "Yes, I'm here. Sorry, I got distracted. How's it all going there?"

"It was going well but I'm afraid I've hit a bit of a snag. It's why I'm trying to contact Jacques. We've lost power to our two levels. The rest of the building is fine, which implies there's an issue with our supply. I've tried to contact the power company, but I don't have the authority to talk to them."

"Oh, I see. Let me think." I rap my knuckles against my forehead. "Have you tried contacting Claude?"

"Yes, but he didn't answer either." His sigh is audible. "I suppose I can wait until Jacques gets home on Sunday, but what if it's a bigger issue and they can't fix it before Monday?"

I draw in a surprised breath and choke on it, coughing a couple of times. Hayden doesn't know? When Jacques said Hayden would be running the business here, I assumed he *knew*.

"Um, Hayden, didn't Jack tell you?"

"Tell me what?"

I curse under my breath. "Uh, he can't make it home on Sunday now." I hear Hayden's surprised gasp and I quickly think of an excuse that won't make Jacques look terrible. "His father passed away this week." At least this is true, Hayden doesn't need to know the sordid details. "He said he was going to call you, but I assume he's got a lot going on."

"Oh, I'm sorry to hear that, I understand but—"

"Yeah, someone should've called you, I'm so sorry they didn't."

He laughs. "I wasn't going to say that. You can't control this sort of situation, it just caught me off guard is all. I've got everything under control for Monday, I just know how much Jacques wanted to be here. I was going to say it doesn't solve the situation *now* and I want everything to be perfect for Monday." He pauses. "Any chance you'd be down as a person permitted to enquire?"

It's a relief that Hayden appears to be an easy-going guy. "I don't know, but it's worth a go. Who's the supplier?"

We hang up after Hayden gives me the details and I make the call. I don't expect to achieve anything, but when they answer and I tell them who I am, they're more than happy to help. Jacques *did* put me down. Ever-organised Jacques. He must've done it before he hired Hayden but didn't think to amend it.

It turns out to be a simple issue, a miscommunication, and once I confirm and approve what's needed, the power is back. While I'm on the call, I make sure to add Hayden to the approver's list.

I give Hayden a call back with the news then stand, brush the sand off my legs, and make my way back to my apartment.

Mum is napping before dinner, so I leave her alone and go into the bedroom. I go over to Jacques' side of the bed and sit on the edge. I open the top drawer of his bedside cupboard and pull out a white t-shirt. I hold it against me and close my eyes as I breathe his faint lingering scent. The tears fall freely as I wonder yet again what went wrong.

I'm reminded of that awkward moment when I first walked in on Jacques talking to his parents in Paris. The first time we broke up because I didn't feel good enough. It might've taken a few months, but we got through it.

This time there's something different. Jacques cutting off the world speaks volumes.

Moe jumps up on the bed and falls asleep against my thigh, his purrs vibrating against it. As I pat him, I absentmindedly sift through Jacques' shirts. Lots of white ones, one or two are black, but they're all plain. He's not a logo or design kinda guy.

When I reach his socks at the bottom, I'm about to put his shirts back when I spot a gap and a box. I reach in and pull it out. It's small, black, and velvet. *A ring box.* My insides swirl with anticipation, heart pounding. Do I dare? *Yes. Do it.*

I open it with trembling hands and gasp. The teardrop diamond glints prettily against the white fabric.

This is *it.* The engagement ring.

Deep down, I always knew this was coming. It was only a matter of when. I had no idea what ring he chose though. It's oh-so-perfect.

No. No, no, no. This is too much.

How long has he had this? And he *still* gave up on us? What the actual hell?

I snap the box shut, scaring Moe in the process who disappears back into the kitchen. I throw the box back in the drawer, throwing Jacques' things on top of it. Anger and confusion vibrate through me as I start pacing the floor, tears coating my cheeks.

Nothing makes any sense. I'm fed up with the lack of communication and the fact that he thinks he should deal with whatever he's going through alone.

Drawing in a shaky breath, I use my hands to wipe the tears away then go to the bathroom to tidy myself up and pull myself together.

It's time to do something I don't normally do. Take action. I vowed I'd fight for him no matter what it takes, and I will. No more sitting back and waiting for someone else to do it for me. Jacques followed me last time. Now it's my turn.

I pick up my phone and send Penny a text.

Call me. ASAP. I need your help.

Chapter 21

Jacques

I am woken by cold air and bright light. Groaning, I grab a pillow and hold it over my face.

"I've been trying to reach you," Claude says, concern evident in his tone. "You didn't come back to work yesterday, you've been ignoring my calls and messages, *and* you were supposed to fly home last night. Jane called Penny, worried sick about you, said you'd ended your relationship. What sort of boneheaded thing is that? What's going on?"

His accusations hit me like daggers and when Claude rips the pillow away, I cover my face with my hands. The memories of Papa's secret and his death, the phone call to Aimée, followed by my phone call to Jane making the biggest mistake of my life, come flooding back with force.

"Go away, Claude." I wish I had never given him a key to my apartment.

"I'm not leaving until I get answers from you."

Claude sits on the edge of the bed. "Come on, man, talk to me. I've never seen you like this. Sabotaging your relationship and your business? This isn't like you."

With a sigh, I sit up and scrub my hands over my face. Looking at Claude I lift my arms in a shrug. "I cannot do it anymore, Claude. I cannot keep pretending everything is okay when it is not."

"What's not okay? You and Jane were fine, weren't you?"

I shuffle to the edge of the bed and swing my legs around, resting my elbows on my thighs, head in hands. "It is not Jane. I was doing her a favour by ending things." I sit up straight and turn to my best friend, but he looks confused. I have not told him about Papa dying, or about my seeing Aimée again, or the big secret for that matter. He knows who Aimée is, we were friends when she was my au pair, but nothing else.

"Come on," Claude slaps my shoulder, "shower, change and let's go and have breakfast somewhere." He glances around my bedroom and wrinkles his nose at the floor covered with takeout containers, glasses that once had cognac in them, and a couple of empty cognac bottles. The living area is worse. I have never lost control like this before, let alone eaten so much takeout. I cannot keep going like this.

"Jacques?" Claude repeats when I do not respond.

I blink a couple of times and nod, knowing he is right. "Fine." On the way to the bathroom, I add by way of an excuse, "I would not have been able to fly home anyway. Last time I checked, all flights were cancelled."

"That was two days ago, Jacques. There's no more snow forecast until Monday or Tuesday. The flights started up again yesterday, you would've made it."

Well, that did not have the effect I intended. My guilt only grows.

⤜⤜⤜ ⤛⤛⤛

The air is still freezing and it stings my cheeks as we walk towards a café we visit often. Our feet crunch on the unmelted snow. Being outdoors again is invigorating and I regret not doing it sooner.

Over coffee and croissants, I tell Claude everything. He is the first person I have spoken to about it and I realise too late I should have done it days ago rather than trying to deal with it myself. I thought I was doing everyone a favour, but I have only proven that sometimes I need help. It is not a sign of weakness, even if it feels it sometimes.

While talking to Rémy and sharing a drink did not fix everything, it did give me peace of mind knowing I did not have to worry about Entreprises DuPont for a few days. Unfortunately, it *does* mean I have sidelined Solutions Exécutives and as a result, I will miss the Gold Coast office opening on Monday.

What have I done?

I am not proud of leaving Hayden in the lurch. In a matter of days, he has proven to be invaluable and I am confident he can handle it, but it was unprofessional of me. I should have told him, but in the end, I forgot all about it.

After I finish talking, I absentmindedly swirl the last dregs of my coffee. "My monster of a father is dead, but I cannot move on from it. My life is a lie, Claude." I gaze into his light brown eyes, thankful that he came when I was at my lowest. He is a good friend and I owe him so much.

But it is not as simple as having coffee and croissants with a friend and everything will be okay again. It is never that simple. How do I move on from this?

Claude finishes his coffee and thinks for a moment. "I understand what you're saying but you can't let this consume you. You can't just give up what you've worked for."

I drink the last of my coffee and place the mug down on the table. "Right now, I do not care about any of that. I gave up Jane because of the stigma of the DuPont name. I cannot look at myself in the mirror, let alone run a business and be a good business partner, and a decent boyfriend to Jane...one day a husband. Or so I hoped."

I think back to the engagement ring I bought. So long ago it feels like an eternity. I left it in Australia, and I chide myself for being so thoughtless. What if Jane finds it? It will be like adding salt to a wound.

"Jane is hurt and confused but if you talk to her, she'll understand," Claude says. "As for the business, you've worked so hard, Jacques. You've put so much time and effort into it, so why waste it? You can't let your past define you. It's the past for a reason. The fact it's a lie shouldn't matter. You're living your life now and writing a better future, the past has no hold over that."

A spark of hope appears in my chest. His words digest as I nod, letting them seep in.

"I need time." I turn to stare out the window. The sky is mostly blue today with tufts of grey clouds. People are out in force enjoying the sunshine while it lasts. I turn back to Claude and add, "Time to process and figure things out."

Claude sighs but nods. "I understand but you can't keep shutting yourself off from the world. If you can't talk to Jane right now that's fine, but don't be alone. At least get back to work, keep busy and show your face online for the opening in Australia."

A small smile tugs at my lips. Keeping busy is good advice. "Alright, Claude, I will do as you say. If Jane calls again, please do not tell her about this...how you found me. Just tell her I am okay."

Claude has a look in his eyes that tells me he disagrees, but all he says is, "Will you call her?"

I hesitate, "I am not sure."

Claude purses his lips but nods once. I appreciate that he does not push me. I can get through this, but it will take time.

Until then, Jane will have to remain a beautiful memory of what could have been. I cannot let her into my life while I am so unstable. I want to be the strong, reliable man she fell in love with. Perhaps in time I will find that side of me again.

⟶⟶⟩ ⟨⟨⟵

On Monday morning I go back into the office as promised. I appeared online at midnight for the Gold Coast opening but I did not go to bed until after two a.m. I am a little sluggish this morning, but that may be from being idle for too long.

So far my morning has consisted of one meeting and two client appointments, many phone calls, and now I have some free time to catch up on my emails before lunch. When I come across an appointment tomorrow with Tavish, my heart constricts. While I turned my phone back on and caught up on my messages and missed calls, there was nothing from Aimée. I must phone her and apologise, but I do not have the courage.

At eleven a.m. there is a knock at the door, and Hugo pokes his head in. "There's someone here to see you."

I bite back a frustrated sigh. "I am busy right now, can they come back?"

Hugo's brows knit together. "I was told to tell you you're going to want to see them."

Them? This time I sigh and shrug in defeat. "Okay, send them in."

I could do with a break from the emails. Getting to my feet, I go over to the window and glance out. Last night the snow returned and today we have a snowstorm. The few people on the streets are rushing to and from their destinations, not wanting to stay out for too long.

As I stare out the window with snow rushing past horizontally, I take in the historical architecture of the city I love. This has been my home for my entire life, but all I want is to go back to one place. A place where I sweat too much, and the humidity makes it hard to breathe. A place where the sunrises are breathtaking and life is laid back and relaxed. A place where my new life was supposed to be...with Jane.

It is easy for Claude to tell me to call her, but I have hurt her. How could she ever forgive me? Besides, I still stand by the fact she deserves better. I made my decision the night Papa died but it will forever be my biggest regret.

A gentle 'ahem' makes me spin around and I am met with deep brown eyes and long, red curly hair tumbling over a young woman's shoulders. I take in her features and my breath catches. She has her mother's face but my father's eyes and nose...like me.

"Avril." The name is foreign to my lips, yet there is no denying it is her even though I have never seen her before. The resemblances are uncanny.

She gasps, her hand flying up to her mouth. "You recognise me?" She has a soft, sweet voice like her mother with an adorable Scottish lilt like Tavish.

Staring at the young woman in my office, my half-sister, I am unable to move. "You look very much like Aimée and you have our Pa—" I clear my throat and change the wording, "—we share the same eyes and nose."

She beams and smiles, looking more like Aimée. She rushes forward and wraps her arms around me, holding me tight. The rush of emotion is unexpected. As I wrap my arms around her slim waist, her soft hair brushing my hands, I experience an unexpected connection to this girl I never knew existed until last week.

Once upon a time I never thought I could connect to anyone so fast, then I met Jane. But what is forming between Avril and me is so different. It is the same thing I am finding with Rémy.

A family bond.

We pull away and I try to inconspicuously dry my tears but Avril is wiping hers too and I give up. We grin at each other and my heart swells with love. I still have a family. It is the most wondrous feeling.

"I am not usually this emotional." I wipe my cheeks with my shirt sleeve.

"Sure, uh huh, I believe you," Avril says with a cheeky grin. "I brought someone with me too."

Before I can do or say anything, Avril rushes to the door and whisper-yells to someone. It takes a little too long for the person to come in and I am not surprised when Aimée appears, keeping her gaze averted. She appears to want to be anywhere but here. She has not forgiven me...not that I blame her.

"This is not necessary," I say, hoping to relieve Aimée's awkwardness, "she does not wish to be here."

Avril's determined gaze meets mine and she purses her lips. "She does, she's just ashamed." She jabs Aimée in the ribs and through clenched teeth says, "Ma, why are you like this? You promised, remember?"

Aimée takes Avril's face in her hands. "I'm sorry, sweetheart. I'm not the best at admitting I'm wrong." Then she turns to me and makes eye contact.

"Tell me about it," Avril mutters.

I half expect to see anger in Aimée's eyes, and I am surprised when it is not there. Instead, she appears contrite. Guilty.

She rushes over and takes my hands, squeezing them tight. "Jacques, I'm so sorry about how I acted on the phone the other night."

My relief is instantaneous. I have never been so happy to be wrong. I open my mouth to tell her I understand, but she holds up her hand, silencing me.

"Don't brush it off as nothing. I was shocked by the news, but it's no excuse for how I behaved. I apologise for being so rude and unkind." She removes one hand from mine and gently strokes my cheek. "You have, and always will mean the world to me. I appreciate what you were trying to do, and it turns out I was wrong." She drops my hands. "I spoke to Avril, and—"

"—Now I'm taking over," Avril interrupts, grabbing Aimée's hand and dragging her to the door. "This is my turn to talk to my brother. I'll meet you and Da in half an hour as planned."

Brother. A warmth grows in my chest and a smile tugs at my lips.

Aimée is practically marched out of my office by Avril, managing a, "Let's have lunch soon," over her shoulder as she leaves.

"Right, let's talk," Avril says when she returns, sitting on a chair in front of my desk.

Going around to the other side of my desk, I sit and nod for her to continue.

"I want the money."

My eyes widen in surprise. I was not expecting that.

"That's not the only reason I'm here by the way," she adds as an afterthought. "It's just Ma told me about the inheritance and it's my choice, right?"

I nod, speechless.

"Right. I've never had much growing up and, like, I appreciate what Ma and Da have given me. Ma is giving me a small lump sum to help start my business, but this inheritance will give it the cash injection it needs to grow."

I open my mouth but Avril steamrolls ahead.

"I love my Ma and she means well, but I can make my own decisions. If I'm entitled to the money, I want it. I'm not going to get hung up on whose it was."

When she pauses for breath, I say, "Okay, but all I ask is you treat this with tact. Your mother told me about the non-disclosure, and while I am not concerned, if it worries her, her identity must be kept hidden."

I make a mental note to research this later. By the time the will is read, I want to be prepared. If anyone is going to challenge it, it will be Maman.

Avril reaches over and squeezes my hand. "The last thing I want to do is hurt Ma. I will be all poise and discreetness." She sits up in her chair and folds her hands in her lap. It lasts all of two seconds before she gasps. "Can I do the sweeping thing?"

"The sweeping thing?"

"Yes. When the will is being read," she jumps up and pretends to open a door, "I *sweep* in," she acts this out too, "and say 'stop the proceedings! I am the forgotten daughter of...of...'" she wrinkles her brow. "What's his name?" she stage whispers.

I laugh despite myself. "Marcel DuPont," I answer, the words sounding bitter.

My half-sister...no, my *sister* is pure sunshine and delight. She already means the world to me, but I fear how she will be affected when her identity comes to light. It may not be for a few months yet, but it is a worry in the back of my mind.

Avril wrinkles her nose. "God, it's so *French*."

I feign hurt. "I take offence to that."

She giggles and plops back down on the chair. I stand and go around the desk to sit on the edge facing her. She turns serious and so do I.

"Are you one hundred per cent sure you want to do this?" I ask.

She swallows, a flash of fear passing across her features before she pulls her shoulders back and holds her head high. "I am not defined by a name, Jacques...no, wait." She wrinkles her nose. "Isn't Jacques the French version of Jack?"

"Yes, it is."

"Would you mind if I called you that instead? It suits you better."

I smile and nod. "I do not mind." I love that it is becoming a special name, only for those close to me.

"Okay, *Jack*," she says with a grin, "I'm not defined by a name. As far as I'm concerned, my father is Tavish Kilpatrick and I am his daughter just without the Scottish blood, but I've got the accent and the red hair, even though it's dyed."

"It is *dyed*?" I asked, astonished.

She rolls her eyes. "Duh, did you think I'd have red hair coming from your and Ma's side of the family?"

I shake my head and shrug. "I suppose not."

She holds out her hair and then lets it fall. "I've been dying it for years but maybe," she smiles at me, "maybe I'll grow it out and try going back to my natural colour. I think we may look more alike." She clears her throat and then gets to her feet. "So, are we doing this?"

"As long as you are sure, then yes. How long are you here for? It may take a while."

She waves my comment away. "I am here indefinitely to help Ma and Da with their shop." She goes over to the window and peers out.

"I am unsure when the will is being read, but I will let you know. I can contact you through your mother I assume?"

She nods, still staring out the window. "Uh, Jack? You better come here."

I get to my feet and join Avril at the window.

"It's snowing hard and there's a woman outside who keeps looking up at this window. She looks cold." Avril frowns up at me.

I glance down at the woman on the snow-covered pavement below and my heart flips inside my chest.

Snowflakes are falling around her. Her long, blonde hair is sticking out of a fluffy beanie, and she's bundled up in a coat, thick trousers, and earmuffs. A picnic basket hangs from her arm, a loaf of French bread wrapped in plastic poking out.

Chapter 22

Jane

C old, cold, cold. So, *freaking* cold.

A shiver runs down my spine, but it only sets off more violent shivering and my teeth start to chatter. I'm wearing all the right gear, but I wasn't expecting it to be *this* cold. Nor did I expect to be standing out in a *snowstorm*.

The change from humid, sunny Gold Coast to this is a huge shock to the system. I can't wait to go back—

No. Rephrase.

It'll be nice to be back in the warmth, *whenever* I can get back.

There. Better.

My focus right now is on saving my relationship with Jacques. I don't care what it takes. If we must stay in Paris, so be it.

In the end I took Mum's advice and left the apartment as it was. I rang Bella the vet who offered to take Moe for a little while. I thought she'd keep him in the cages at the vet surgery, but she's taking him home and that puts my mind at ease knowing he won't be alone. I'm not giving up that fluff ball. If Jacques and I work things out—no *when* we work things out—he won't forgive me if I give up Moe. Hell, *I* wouldn't forgive myself.

If we stay here indefinitely, I'll make other plans.

I shift the picnic basket to my other arm and peer up at the building again, trying to remember which window is Jacques' office. Is it the one on the left near the edge of the building? Or is it closer to the centre? I have no clue. I never paid much attention. Shuffling from foot to foot in a futile attempt to keep warm, I remove my phone from my pocket for the umpteenth time. Still nothing from Claude.

If he doesn't reply or come out in the next minute, I'm leaving before I turn into an icicle. There's a quaint little coffee shop not far from here and I will make a beeline for it.

I send off one more annoyed text, using all caps for emphasis.

WHERE ARE YOU? I'M FREEZING TO DEATH OUT HERE!

I pocket my phone again.

This morning has not gone to plan *at all*. I arrived last night, making it before the snowstorm. I'm staying with Claude and Penny and I was sure our plan for me to surprise Jacques was foolproof. I was going to entice him to a long lunch so we could enjoy the picnic outdoors, semi-reliving our first date at Île de la Cite. It was all dependent on it not snowing.

Claude and Penny were sort of essential to the plan in case Jacques put up too much resistance. I still don't know much about what he's been going through, but they told me there is reason to worry he may not want to see me.

Yeah, that hurts. A *lot*. But it doesn't deter me.

Penny and I were going to come in together. Claude would tell Jacques that Penny was here and I'd tag behind and surprise him.

Of course, nothing is going to plan.

First problem: Snowstorm. Snow was forecast for later today but it came early in the form of a storm, surprising everyone. It's not a blizzard yet, but it's darn close.

Second problem: The babysitter fell through. This shouldn't have been a problem as Penny could've taken the kids with her. But, you know, the snowstorm sorta put a spanner in the works. Apparently taking kids out in this weather is not recommended.

Noted for future reference. Because, trust me, I'd do something that stupid.

In the end I had to do this on my own. When I turned up, I texted Claude but when he didn't reply after five minutes, I rang the intercom on the building. The new security guard, who hasn't met me, wouldn't let me in. Now I'm standing in the street freezing my boobs off.

Still nothing from Claude. I consider turning away when the automatic doors slide open, but Jacques runs out. He stops for a second, looking around, before finally looking at me. Our gazes meet.

He's here!

My breath catches and my heart starts beating frantically. This is it.

It's almost slo-mo as he advances towards me, his dark hair catching on the wind and snowflakes landing on it. This may not be going to plan, but hey, I can still surprise him.

A smile blossoms on my face as I stand tall, tears stinging my eyes. Waiting with bated breath for the long-awaited kiss. Or hug. Either would be nice.

It's going to be so romantic. He'll apologise, I'll apologise, and we'll kiss in the snow. Just like we did at our little—okay *long*—walk.

When he stops in front of me, I can feel his warmth and I breathe in his scent which is oh-so-familiar now. My bottom lip wobbles as I say, "Jack—" even managing a little pucker as I wait for that long-awaited reunion.

"What are you doing?" he chides, wrapping his arm around my shoulders and practically manhandling me into the building.

Let down much?

"Jack—"

Too focused on getting me out of the storm, he ignores me. I'm grateful for the escape from the cold, I should add, but he's got blinkers on.

"Why are you standing in the snowstorm?" he snaps as we pass through the doors. "You are frozen."

The warmth of the building makes my face sting but, oh, the relief!

"I—"

"What are you doing here?" His gaze meets mine, a range of emotions raging in their brown depths.

I open my mouth to respond but this time I don't get to say anything.

"No, do not answer. You should not be here." He rips his gaze away and shakes his head. His shoulders are tight, his posture rigid. Geez, I wasn't expecting this much resistance.

Frustrated, I huff out a sigh and after dropping the basket on the floor, I reach up to grab his face in my gloved hands, forcing him to look at me. "Jack, can I talk? Please?"

His resistance wanes and when his gaze meets mine, his eyes have lost their hardness. Vulnerabilities flood in, along with some tears. Why, oh why did he shut me out? What's going through that head of his? We've come so far with being open with each other, I don't understand what's changed.

His face falls and he, *finally*, bundles me in his arms and hugs me so tight I can't breathe. But I don't care. I don't care *at all*. Because I'm where I want and need to be. I meld into his hard chest, welcoming his warmth and closeness once again.

"You should not be here," he whispers in my ear. "But I am so happy."

I pull back and hold a gloved finger against his lips. "My turn to talk, okay?"

He sighs and takes a step back, letting me go. He scrubs a hand down his face. I only now notice he's wearing a flimsy long-sleeved shirt. He must be freezing.

"Let's go upstairs first. Claude assured me you had a free block about now."

He narrows his eyes. "I should have known Claude had something to do with this."

I narrow my eyes in return. "Only because he cares about you, and so do I. Now—"

"Jack!"

I spin around and watch in surprise as a beautiful, young redhead races up to Jacques and kisses his cheek before embracing him. I almost turn green with envy, and I'm not the jealous type. I trust Jacques, but this green-eyed monster deep down is taunting me, and I don't like it. *At all.*

She pulls back and beams at him. "I'm sorry but I must go and meet Ma and Da for lunch." She holds out her phone, "Give me your phone number and I'll text you."

My mouth gapes open when Jacques takes the phone. The girl glances over, seeing me for the first time, and gives me a bright smile. She doesn't even care that she's hitting on my boyfriend. Does she not know who I am? Gosh, I sound so pompous, yet I still pull my shoulders back and scowl at her. She doesn't see it though as she turns back to Jacques.

When Jacques hands her phone back, she types a message and pockets her phone.

"You should have my number now. I'm so glad we got to meet, keep in touch about how things go with the will." She embraces him once more and throws me a little smile before dashing out into the snow.

The will? I glance at Jacques, eyebrows raised. "Going younger, are we?" I try to make it sound like a joke but I hear the accusation in my tone. It's not intentional but I can't control it.

Jacques' eyes grow wide. "What? No!" He huffs. "It is not what you think."

I grin, pick up the basket, and take his hand with my free one. "It's a good thing I trust you, hey? Now come on, let's go have some food and you can talk to me. No point in talking while you're hangry."

We stop at the elevators, and I press the button.

Jacques stares at me blankly and shakes his head, baffled. "Even after all this time you manage to surprise me. What is this word *hangry*?"

The elevator doors open, and I chuckle as we step inside, my knotted stomach starting to loosen. Jacques presses the button to his floor.

"It's two words mashed into one. 'Hungry' and 'Angry'. Hangry." I grin at him and a flood of relief rushes over me when the tiniest hint of a smile tugs at his lips.

He sighs and rakes a hand through his hair, the last few unmelted snowflakes drifting to the elevator floor.

"Jane," he says with a sigh, "I cannot let you—"

"Jack," I turn to him, "I'm a big girl and I can handle whatever it is you're going through. You can't get rid of me that easily."

"I am trying to protect you." His jaw is clenched and twitching.

"I don't need protecting, Jack." I look at him hard but he stares straight ahead, refusing to make eye contact. This is stressing him out and while I appreciate that he cares so much, I've got to find a way to stop him from being so damn stubborn and listen to me. I'm not going to run away.

I love him, but when he gets like this it annoys the hell out of me. I'm just glad I brought food, the whole 'a way to a man's heart is through his stomach' thing is so true when it comes to Jacques.

The tension between us grows on the way up to his floor. When the doors open with a ding, cool air rushing in, I can breathe again. Stepping out, I glance into a room where Claude happens to be sitting at the head of the table conducting a meeting. He must sense me looking and his head snaps up, eyes widening. He glances down at his phone and back up at me, mouthing 'sorry'. I smile to tell him it's okay and follow Jacques to his office.

When we arrive, he sits at his desk and I go in after him, shutting the door and removing my coat, gloves, and earmuffs, dumping them on the floor. Grabbing the picnic basket, I set it on his desk and start unpacking.

He watches as I take everything out, his expression changing when he realises I've replicated our first date.

He meets my gaze and gives me a small smile. "Thank you." He reaches out and takes my left hand, leaning in to kiss it. His lips land on the promise ring and he stares at it for a long moment before looking up at me with tear-filled eyes. "I am sorry," he whispers, kissing it again.

Finally, a breakthrough.

Moving the basket onto the floor, over a delicious *charcuterie* we talk.

❧❧❧ ❧❧❧

We finish the food in record time and we both listen as we reveal what we've been through this past week or so.

"Oh Jack," I reach across for his hands, "I'm so sorry."

"I am sorry too," he says, squeezing my hands.

I wish that he'd talked to me earlier, it could've saved so much heartache. But I also understand that overwhelming desire to flee and protect everyone around you.

"But for what it's worth, I'm still not going anywhere," I add. "I love you, Jack. If we're going to make this work, it involves being together through the good times and the bad."

"But how can I let you be a part of my evil family?"

"You don't have to *let* me, Jack. Isn't it my decision?"

Jacques glares at me hard. I can tell he wants to say no because he's stubborn, but he also knows that he cannot make my decisions for me.

"Life will not be easy with me. My family will not be going anywhere."

"I don't care." I stand and go around to him, leaning against the desk.

"My father did some terrible things."

"I know, and I'm sorry, but you have a beautiful sister because of it."

I cringe, embarrassed at my little moment earlier. If I hadn't been so emotional and irrational, I would've seen the resemblances.

"You will be tainted by my name," Jacques says.

"Who says I have to take your name?" I move to straddle him, wrapping my arms around his neck. "You could always take mine."

Jacques wrinkles his nose. "Jacques Collins...Jack Collins." He shakes his head. "No, that does not work. I used to be proud of my name."

I grin at him, remembering our very first meeting. "Trust me, I remember." Clearing my throat, I emphasise a terrible French accent, "My name is Jacques, Jacques DuPont. My name is strong, *non*?"

He breaks out into a full-on grin and wraps his arms around me, holding me close to him.

I lean in so our lips are only inches apart, his warm breath fanning my face. "I quite like your name. But if it bothers you that much, I guess I'll forever be a Collins. But it's a shame, Jane DuPont has a nice ring to it."

Jacques' eyes smoulder. "It does, I agree. But—"

Unable to hold back, I press my lips to his in a swift, passionate kiss.

I pull away and gaze into his eyes. "Jack, I'm a shameless traditionalist and I *want* to take your name. I don't care about some stupid stigma, and it's *not* cursed." I shake my head. "A name doesn't define a person, it's *just* a name."

Jacques thinks for a moment. "You sound like Avril. While I appreciate the sentiment, in business a name can make or break it."

"Yes, but you've already proven you and your business are different. You can, and should, be proud of that. I'll only be defined by *you*, not your family."

Jacques sighs. "Why are you always right?"

"Because I'm a woman, we're always right."

He chuckles. "Rémy and I have been getting to know each other. He is not so bad. I will help him with the business, train him to be a good leader."

I look at him proudly. "That's great!"

He sighs. "Maman and Céleste will never be far away with Entreprises DuPont in my name."

I shrug again. "So be it. I will accept Rémy into our home with open arms, and I will do my best to get on with your Mum and Céleste."

Jacques reaches out to stroke my cheek, his eyes showing his gratitude. "Thank you. I am glad you are here, Jane. I am sorry, for everything."

"No more apologies. You were going through a difficult time. I would never hold that against you. All I ask is next time don't shut me out. We need to work through these difficult times together. Okay?"

He nods without hesitation, tightening his grip around me. "I still want our life to be in Australia, but it may just take a while longer."

"I don't care. I'll have to go home for a little while, for Mum's surgery but she won't let me stay for the treatment. She's more concerned about us working things out."

"I would like to come back with you if that is okay. I would like to support you and your family."

Warmth spreads through me as I smile and nod. "I would love that, and so would Mum. The doctor is confident, and Mum is very positive, which will help her recovery."

Checking the time, I realise it's close to one p.m. I slide off his lap and remember one last thing.

"I'll let you get back to work, but before I do..." I go over to my bag and retrieve the ring box, taking it back to Jacques with a sheepish smile. "I stumbled across this by accident. I confess all it did was reinforce that I wasn't going to let you destroy us."

His gaze drops to the ring box then back up at me. "I am sorry you found it at such a difficult time but thank you. For believing in us." He takes the box and puts it in his drawer, locking it. "I still want to do this properly. Do you trust me?"

"With my life, Jack."

And on those words, I know we're going to be okay. We're going to have to work hard at our relationship, but doesn't everyone? Whatever it takes, I will forever fight for us no matter where we are. Australia, France, or anywhere else, I no longer care.

As long as we're together.

Also in This Series

Lonely in Paris is the first book in the series. A fun, lighthearted, billionaire romance set in the City of Love.

Jane's #1 rule in Paris: Don't fall in love

After ending a disastrous relationship, Jane accepts a job in the City of Love. The trouble is she speaks very little French, has no friends to enjoy Paris with, and she's awfully lonely.

Then she meets Jacques DuPonot.

Rich, handsome, and the cream of the Parisian crop, Jacques is living the dream. Just not his own. His father wants him to follow in his footsteps, but Jacques wants to earn his success. Trapped in a life chosen by his family, he's always been alone.

Until he meets Jane.

He's from money. She's not.
He's a planner. She's impulsive.
He's serious. She's *definitely* not.

They couldn't be more different, but they will fall. Hard.

Together Jane and Jacques will learn why Paris is the City of Love. But when an expiring visa, a jealous colleague, and manipulative family threaten their fledgling relationship, their loyalties will be tested to breaking point.

Jane broke her #1 rule, now they must decide what they are willing to sacrifice for love.

Navigate to the URL below to purchase this book.

https://books2read.com/LonelyinParis

Finding Our Home, the third book in this series concludes Jane and Jacques' story. Available for pre-order now.

https://books2read.com/FindingOurHome

Other Books by Lisa Stanbridge

Abandoned Hearts is my debut novel. A heartfelt story about two broken individuals who must learn to trust again.

Finally free from her abusive ex, Claire Stone accepts a job as a live-in nurse in the small beach-side town of Busselton, Western Australia. A new life is exactly what she needs. Move away, move on, forget. If only things were that simple. Even the intriguing but abrasive son of her new patient can't shield her from relentless memories.

Michael Karalis is watching his mother die while battling his ex-wife for custody of his five year old son. He's bitter, broken, and distrustful, but Claire becomes a light in his world, despite his reservations. Two broken souls need to learn to trust again and open their hearts or they'll never find the love they both need.

Navigate to the URL below to purchase this book.

https://books2read.com/AbandonedHearts

Acknowledgments

Thank you for reading **Troubled in Paradise**. I hope you enjoyed it.

Queensland, especially the Gold Coast, has always held a special place in my heart. The first time I visited towards the end of 1998, I was still a teenager and it was my first time visiting Queensland *and* my first time flying on a plane. It was all new and exciting. I remember waking up one morning and the sun was shining brightly so I got up and showered. It wasn't until I went downstairs that I noticed it wasn't even 6 a.m.! Queensland doesn't observe daylight savings and their sunrises are very early in spring.

This was my first taste of Queensland and my love of it only grew. I don't like the humidity, but everything else is perfection. Stunning scenery. Lots of sunshine. Friendly people. The amazing beaches. The easy way of life. I can't recommend it enough. When I first decided to make this into a series, I knew one book had to have the Gold Coast as the hub. I'm very excited to be going back in May 2023.

I've always wanted to live there but it never eventuated. I tried for about a month or two after I graduated high school but I was young and unskilled, so getting work was hard. In the end, I had to go back home to South Australia and eventually found a job elsewhere, so my dream of living in Queensland never happened. But it did become a regular holiday destination and I've got many fond memories.

As for the writing of this story, the usual people require so many thanks. I hope they all know they're going to be acknowledged in every book because they all mean so much to me and they need to know they're appreciated.

Pete, my amazing husband, and proofreader. Ever since I started this indie journey, he's thrown his full support behind me and believes in me when I don't believe in myself. He never holds back in giving me brutal feedback on my stories, too, which I LOVE.

Frances Dall'Alba, my fabulous critique partner. Another person I can rely on for honesty. Thank you so much for everything. I can only imagine how frustrating it must get when I send revised chapters for you to reread, or when there are weeks with no chapters because I'm busy, blocked, or stuck rewriting a plot hole. Thanks for being so patient!

My amazing beta readers, you know who you are.

And last but not least, all the countless people who have offered advice or shared knowledge with me.

Thank you all!

About the Author

International award-winning Australian author Lisa Stanbridge has been writing ever since she could string sentences together. As a child, it started off with princesses in castles being rescued by Prince Charming. As a teenager she moved on to angsty teens struggling through life with raging hormones. Now, as a semi-mature adult, she writes sweet contemporary romances and romantic comedies about real people going through real struggles who want their HEA.

She has been shortlisted in many contests, and even won some! Her biggest award is for her debut novel, **Abandoned Hearts**, which won 'Best First Book' in the Koru Award of Excellence, run by Romance Writers of New Zealand.

When she's not writing, Lisa works full time as a Software Tester. She reads anything she can sink her teeth into, and loves binging on

TV shows, especially the British ones. Lisa loves lazy days at the beach reading or writing, but rarely swimming, and loves spending time with her husband and her friends.

Say hello to Lisa

Visit her website and subscribe to her newsletter. It will keep you up to date with:

- New releases

- Preorder links

- New cover reveals and excerpts

And lots more!

https://lisastanbridge.wixsite.com/lisastanbridgeauthor

Leave a review

Did you enjoy this book? The best favour you can do for an author is to leave a review. If you'd like to leave one, go to your place of purchase, or search for the book on Goodreads, Amazon, or BookBub and leave a review. Thank you.